D0292233

GOBLIN SECRETS

GOBLIN SECRETS

William Alexander

MARGARET K. MCELDERRY BOOKS
New York London Toronto Sydney New Delhi

MARGARET K. McELDERRY BOOKS

An imprint of Simon & Schuster Children's Publishing Division

1230 Avenue of the Americas, New York, New York 10020

MARGARET K. McELDERRY BOOKS is a trademark of Simon & Schuster, Inc.

For information about special discounts for bulk purchases, please contact Simon & Schuster Special Sales at 1-866-506-1949 or business@simonandschuster.com.

The Simon & Schuster Speakers Bureau can bring authors to your live event. For more information or to book an event, contact the Simon & Schuster Speakers Bureau at 1-866-248-3049 or visit our website at www.simonspeakers.com.

Book design by Debra Sfetsios-Conover

The text for this book is set in Adobe Caslon.

Manufactured in the United States of America

1112 FFG

10 9 8 7 6 5 4 3

Library of Congress Cataloging-in-Publication Data

Alexander, William (William Joseph), 1976–

Goblin secrets / William Alexander.—1st ed.

p. cm.

Summary: Hoping to find his lost brother, Rownie escapes the home of the witch Graba and joins a troupe of goblins who perform in Zombay, a city where humans are forbidden to wear masks and act in plays.

ISBN 978-1-4424-2726-6 (hardcover)

ISBN 978-1-4424-2728-0 (eBook)

[1. Fantasy. 2. Magic—Fiction. 3. Goblins—Fiction. 4. Entertainers—Fiction. 5. Masks—Fiction. 6. Missing persons—Fiction. 7. Brothers—Fiction.] I. Title.

PZ7.A3787Gob 2012

[E]—dc23

2011015491

for Liam

GOBLIN SECRETS

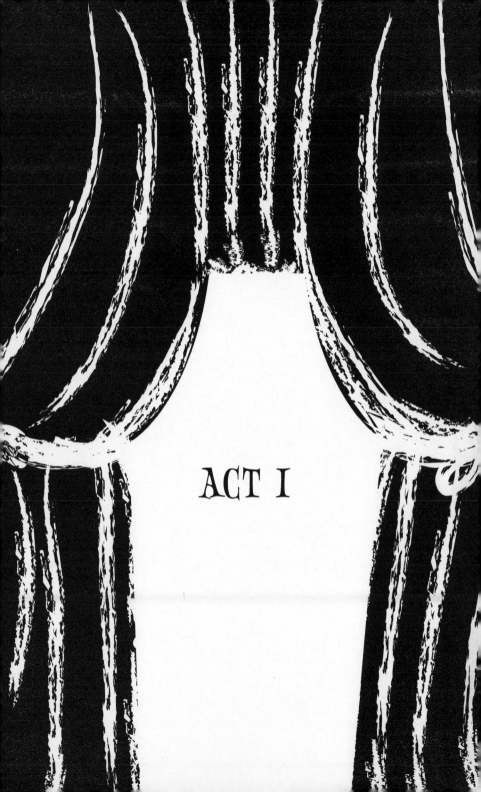

ACT I

Act I, Scene I

ROWNIE WOKE WHEN GRABA knocked on the ceiling from the other side. Plaster dust drifted down from the knocking. Graba knocked again. Baskets hung on chains from the rafters, and they shook when she knocked.

Rownie sat up and tried to blink sleep-sand and plaster dust from one eye. The whole floor was covered by a bed made up of straw, stolen clothes sewn into blankets, and sleeping siblings. Two of his brothers crawled up out of the straw, Blotches and Stubble. Blotches had orange hair, orange freckles, and orange teeth. Stubble was the oldest and the tallest, and he liked to say that he had a beard. He didn't. He had stray hairs on the tip of his chin and on his cheeks near his ears.

Their sister Vass came in from the girls' room, which was really the same room with a blanket hung across the middle. Vass had been her name before she came to live with Graba. Sometimes Graba's grandchildren kept the names they had before. Sometimes they made up names for themselves. Blotches and Stubble had made up their own names.

"Hurry," Vass snapped.

Rownie got to his feet, combed the straw out of his hair with his fingers, and stumbled away from the middle of the room. He stood with Vass and Blotches while Stubble pulled the rope that lowered the stairway down from the ceiling. The musty smell of Graba's loft came down with it.

Vass went upstairs. The others followed her. Rownie came last.

There were birds everywhere in Graba's loft. Most were pigeons, gray and mangy. Some were chickens. A few larger, stranger birds perched in dark corners, watchful.

Graba perched on a stool near the iron stove, her legs hidden underneath the bulk of her gray skirts.

"Four grandchildren," she said. "Today I have four of you. Enough for what I have in mind now."

The word "*grandmother*" did not mean "mother's mother" or "father's mother" to Rownie, or to the various other children who sometimes lived in Graba's shack. Neither mothers nor fathers were part of this household, and the word "*grandmother*" simply meant "Graba."

The four children lined up in front of the stool, waiting.

Two chickens pecked at the floorboards nearby, looking for seeds.

"I'll need eggs carried to Haggot's market stall," said Graba. She pointed to Stubble and Blotches, but she did not say their names. She probably did not know their names. "He'll be at the Northside market today. Trade the eggs for feed-grain, the best chicken feed you can find. Bring it back to me. Will you do that, now?"

"Yes, Graba." Stubble picked up a wooden crate filled with straw and eggs. All four siblings turned to go.

"Don't be going yet," Graba said. She took a small leather bag from around her neck and held it out to Vass. "Hang this over the chains on the Clock Tower door. Sing the charm I was teaching you last night, and stand back when you do. Take care with this, now. It is a present of welcoming home, and it's almost ripe."

Vass took the bag carefully. "What's in it?" she asked.

"A bird skull, stuffed with other things. Do this well, and I might be teaching you the making of it."

"Yes, Graba," said Vass.

"Go," Graba said. "All of you but the runt, the smallest one. Rownie should wait here with me."

Rownie waited. He wondered why Graba knew *his* name. She knew the names of those she kept an eye on, and it was not always a good thing to have Graba's eye on you.

He listened to Vass, Stubble, and Blotches clamber down the stairs.

"Yes, Graba?" Rownie asked.

"My leg bones have run down," she told him. "Wind them for me now." She extended a gearwork leg from under her stool. It was bird-shaped, with three long talon-toes in front and one in back, at the heel. The whole limb had been made out of copper and wood.

Rownie pried the crank out from her shin and wound it up, watching gears turn against chains and springs inside.

* * *

Graba always said that Mr. Scrud, the local gearworker, hadn't enough skill to make legs into human shapes. Vass whispered that Graba needed the chicken legs to hold up her hugeness, that nothing smaller would suffice, and that Graba wouldn't be able to walk today if she hadn't lost the ordinary legs she'd been born with.

Stubble said that Graba used to be a sailor, or a boat-witch, and that she'd lost her legs in a pirate attack. He said Graba killed some of the pirates with a look and a laugh and a lock of her hair before they cut off her legs with rusty swords. He always drew out the word "rusty" when he told the story. "Rrrrrrrusty swords. Ha!" Then he'd hit Rownie behind the knee with a stick to buckle him over.

Stubble told this story often. Rownie had cried the first

time, and the rest of Graba's grandchildren had laughed. On the second telling Rownie had glared up at Stubble from the ground. The third time Stubble told the tale Rownie had fallen backward on purpose, throwing up his hands and imitating Graba's rusty voice. "Curse you, Pirate King!" (The story had grown by then, and the ordinary river pirates had become a full barge captained by the King of All Pirates.)

Everybody had laughed. Stubble had helped him up, and after that he didn't hit Rownie so hard while telling the pirate story, because Rownie couldn't say his line if he was gasping in pain and holding his leg. It still hurt, but not as much.

Now the story was almost a play. This was dangerous. Performances were outlawed in Zombay.

* * *

Rownie finished turning the left crank as far as it would go and folded it into the shin. Graba pulled back her left leg and then extended her right. Rownie pried out the crank and turned it once. The joint gave a loud, shrill creaking. Graba waved her hands and scowled.

"Needs oil," she said. She reached up into the rafters and into one of the nests. She plucked out a small brown egg and popped it into her mouth. It crunched. "I haven't any gear oil left," she said around the cracking eggshell.

"Get to Scrud's shop for a small flask, now. I've overpaid him for leg repair, and he owes me for it. Don't let him tell you otherwise."

"Yes, Graba," Rownie said. He folded back the crank, dodged around a chicken, and ran down the stairs.

He grabbed his coat, even though it was a little too warm outside for coats, and tried to leave through the door. The door wouldn't budge. Rownie remembered that it couldn't budge. Graba moved her house around sometimes. She would send everyone out, lift up the shack, and go somewhere else. Then she would let everyone back in after they found her, if they ever did find her. The last time Graba moved her house, she set the front door against a neighboring wall. "Just use a window," she had said when Vass complained. "I like my view better this way."

Rownie climbed through the window and dropped down to the street.

Act I, Scene II

THE SOUTH SIDE OF THE CITY was dusty. Rownie tried not to step in any of the dust piles that littered the street. Every morning sweepers swept their houses, and they left large, brown piles outside their doorsteps. Every day the dust came slowly back inside and covered the floors. There was a kind of fish that swam in Southside dust, and a kind of bird that fished with their long beaks in the dust dunes. The lives of sweepers became interesting during dustfish spawning season.

Rownie pulled on his coat, which was very much too big for him. It was dust colored, or else so covered with dust that the coat couldn't remember any other color. He wished that Graba had sent him to the market with the others rather than to Mr. Scrud's gear shop. He was hungry. Graba never fed her household, but she usually sent them on food-errands. The others would buy bread and pastries for themselves, as well as the chicken feed, and eat on their way home. They probably wouldn't save him any, and Rownie couldn't sip gear oil on his own way home. This errand wouldn't feed him.

He kicked over a dust pile beside the rusting gate to the old rail station, and then coughed and wished he hadn't.

The street Rownie picked his way down did not run in a straight line. He walked underneath houses built on top of each other, with newer rooms and houses added on stilts or jutting out sideways and held in place by thick lengths of chain. Tin roofs, thatched roofs, and wooden shingles leaned over his head, almost touching across the width of the road.

Rownie was not very tall, but others on the street made way for him. People always made way for those who were Graba's.

He came to the Fiddleway Bridge.

Two fiddlers stood at either side of the entrance. They played dueling tunes at each other. Hats rested on the stones in front of them, and both hats were half full of coins.

Rownie scooped up a pebble from the ground, just like he always did when he crossed the Fiddleway. This one was gray, with an orange line running through the middle of it. He carried it with him through the entranceway, through the crossfire of dueling music, and onto the bridge.

The Fiddleway was wide, and long enough to disappear

into the fog of a foggy day. The central avenue had been cobbled together several times out of old stone and new ironworks. Small shops and apartments stood on both sides, separated by alleyways that looked out over the expanse of the Zombay River.

Rownie passed musicians of several sorts, and empty hats reserving spots for musicians who were not yet there. He passed piles of horse dung and cow dung and other kinds of dung that he wasn't sure about, but the smell wasn't so bad as on the Southside roads. River winds kept the air clean on the bridge. He made sure his coat didn't drag in any of the dung piles.

Several members of the Guard came marching toward Rownie, with their Captain in the lead. Rownie could tell that the Guard Captain had decided not to notice him, but he waited longer than he should have before moving aside. He knew they couldn't detain him here on the Fiddleway. The bridge was a sanctuary. No one ever got arrested while still on the bridge. Rownie figured that most of the houses here had been built by smugglers and other sorts of people who couldn't set foot in the city, on either side.

The Guard Captain tried to glare at Rownie and ignore him at the same time. He had an impressive glare. Every member of the Guard had gearworked legs, and some of them also had gearworked arms, but only the Captain had eyes made of tiny glass gears with dark stained-glass irises. Each iris was gear-shaped. They rotated slowly within the workings of his eyes.

Boots struck the bridge at perfectly regular intervals as they marched. The Guard always marched. The way their legs were made, they had no other option but to march.

"May your feet fall off," Rownie whispered to the backs of them, once they had all passed. "May your breath smell like pigeon feathers." He tried to chant the words, to make them into a proper curse, to make them stick. He wished he knew how to curse better. Graba knew excellent curses, of course, but she only shared their secrets with Vass.

In the very center of the bridge stood the Clock Tower of Zombay. A stained-glass sun climbed up the stained-glass sky of the clock face, high above the etched glass horizon of the cityscape. The face glinted, bright with reflected sunlight. When the real sun set overhead, the glass sun in the clock would set behind the glass horizon. Then, at nightfall, lanterns would light up behind the clock face and the miniature glass moon as it ticked its way across the sky.

The whole of Zombay was very proud of its clock, though the tower was said to be haunted by clockmaker ghosts. The big front doors were latched, locked, and chained shut. No one ever went inside.

Vass stood by the tower doors with her back to the road, chanting over Graba's charm bag. Rownie did not interrupt her, though he did wonder why Graba would want to tie a gift of welcoming home to the Clock Tower. No one lived in the Clock Tower.

He continued on his way, looking for one particular stretch of low stone wall, and there he found Stubble and Blotches. They had the crate of eggs with them. They were sitting exactly where Rownie always threw pebbles over the wall's side. Rownie didn't want them to be there, but there they were.

They saw him. Blotches took an egg from the crate and offered it to him. Rownie reached for it, because he was hungry, even though he knew that Blotches never gave anybody anything.

Blotches snatched the egg back and tossed it into the River.

Rownie cried out.

Stubble smacked Blotches on the top of his head. "Don't waste food," he said. "Not ever." He looked over at Rownie. Rownie hoped that he'd offer another egg, but he didn't. "Did you wind up her ankle?" Stubble asked. Rownie started to answer, but Blotches talked right over him. Blotches had large ears, round and ruddy, but he never used them for much.

"You missed the goblins," Blotches said.

"What goblins?" Rownie asked.

"They came by in a tinker's-wagon," said Stubble.

"One of them had long, metal teeth, sticking out all over," said Blotches.

"Did not," said Stubble.

"Did so. I threw an egg at that one."

"She caught the egg and threw it back at you. And those weren't metal teeth. Those were nails. She used one to hang up a sign."

"Did not."

"She did. She was just holding the nails in her mouth to keep both hands free."

"Maybe they use metal teeth for nails," said Blotches. "Maybe they grow them back as fast as they can pluck them out."

"You're a kack," said Stubble.

"What did the sign say?" Rownie asked, but they ignored him. They probably didn't know.

"Vass should be done with the door by now," Stubble said, changing the subject, but Rownie didn't want to change the subject.

"I didn't know goblins could come out in daylight," Rownie said.

"They have to keep moving if they do," said Blotches.

"Goblins never have a home, any of them. That's why they live in wagons. The sun finds them out and burns up any building they stay in for longer than a day and a night. That's why they're never goldsmiths, too, because it's sun-metal. They're only tinsmiths. And iron burns them."

"Liar," said Stubble. "They don't work with iron because it's too hard and heavy. Tin's easier."

"And they're thieves," said Blotches, as though the other one had just agreed with him.

"Obviously," said Stubble.

"What do they steal?" Rownie asked.

"Everything," said Blotches.

"The smallest child in every family," added Stubble. "That's why Graba only sends the oldest of us with tin pots for mending. No one ever sends a small child to the wagons unless they don't mean for them to come back." He snickered, three quick snorts of laughter forced out of his nose instead of his mouth.

"Liar," Rownie said.

"It's true," said Blotches. "And they eat the children they steal."

He started singing a song about thieving goblins. Rownie turned away and looked at the pebble in his hand. "Hello," he said, whispering low so the other two couldn't hear him, and then he threw it as far as he could. The rock made a small splash when it hit the River, but the waters did not otherwise react.

Stubble stopped singing and smacked the side of Rownie's head. "Don't get the River's attention," he said. "The floods will come for you."

Rownie rubbed his head with one hand. He didn't look up. He watched the River. It was vast, and Rownie couldn't look at it for long. There was too much of it to take in. He watched until he had to look away, and then he looked at the ravine walls to either side of the River, and after that he looked at the stones in front of him.

Rownie had a brother older than any of the siblings who shared Graba's shack, an actual birth-brother. They looked alike, both of them dark with dark eyes—eyes you couldn't easily see the bottom of. Everyone called the brothers Rowan and Little Rowan. After a while "Little Rowan" shortened into "Rownie." Rownie had never had a name of his own. Their mother drowned before she'd had a chance to name him.

He also didn't know how old he was. Vass kept saying that Rownie was eight years old. She remembered everyone's birthday, but she didn't always tell the truth about birthdays, and Rownie suspected that she was lying about his. He was sure he was closer to ten.

Rownie and Rowan used to throw pebbles together,

right on this spot on the Fiddleway Bridge. They would listen to the musicians, and Rowan would tell stories about the River and about their mother; how she had skippered a barge and gone down with it just underneath the Fiddleway. Only Rowan was able to swim to shore. He carried Rownie with him.

Vass didn't believe that story. *No one can swim through that part of the River*, she would argue. *The currents are too strong. You would have drowned too.* Rowan only shrugged. *We didn't drown*, was all the answer he gave.

Later, he showed Rownie where to toss pebbles down from the bridge. *We drop the stones to say hello. It's like leaving a small pile of stones on a grave. The dead speak in stones. Pebbles are the proper way to tell them hello.* So Rownie always said hello when he crossed the bridge, even though he didn't remember his mother at all, or her barge, or a time before Rowan brought him to stay with Graba because they didn't have anywhere else to stay.

Rowan had been gone for a couple of months now. Stubble, Blotches, and the rest seemed to have forgotten about him already—but Graba remembered. *If you hear from your brother*, she'd say, *you'll be sure to tell Graba, now. A charmer, that one. Your Graba misses her grandchildren, all of her grandchildren, and that one she worries for.*

Rownie had never known Graba to worry about anyone,

and Rowan hadn't even slept in Graba's shack for over a year. He was too old—sixteen years old—and he took up too much of the straw floor when he slept there. Still, Rownie nodded and promised to tell Graba if he heard from his brother.

You will do that, now, Graba agreed.

Stubble and Blotches started up a song about floodwaters and falling bridges, which seemed to Rownie a very stupid thing to sing about while actually on a bridge. He left them there and crossed the road, looking for the goblin sign—and looking for some sign of Rowan, just like he always did on the Fiddleway. He found the goblin sign, but only the goblin sign. It had been tacked to the opposite railing with one iron nail. Rownie read it carefully. He was good at reading. Rowan had taught him how. It read:

THEATRE!

A Troupe of Tamlin PLAYERS will Delight and
Astound the Citizens of this
Fair City at Dusk.

Discover their Stage in the CITY
FAIRGROUNDS.

The stage will be Illuminated by Cunning Devices.

The Players will present the finest
Performances of MIMICRY, MUMMERY, and
VERSE,

along with Feats of Musical and Acrobatic Skill to
Delight every Eye and Ear.

Two Coppers per Audience Member.

He read it again. He still didn't believe it. He read it again.

Goblins were putting on a play. Nobody could put on a play. Nobody was allowed to put on a play, but goblins were going to. Maybe he could see some of the show before they all got arrested.

Rownie ran the rest of the way across the bridge, through music from fiddles and whistles and drums. His coat billowed behind him like a sail.

Act I, Scene III

BROKEN GEARS AND STACKS OF WOOD filled the alleyway outside Scrud's workshop. Rownie heard shouting inside. He waited in the alley and rooted through some of the mess of gears until the shouting faded to a low mutter. Then he went in.

The noise did not actually stop. It never did. Mr. Scrud was always shouting to himself.

"Hello, Mr. Scrud!" Rownie called out from the doorway, hoping to be noticed now rather than later. The workshop smelled like sawdust and oil, with a rotten smell underneath. Scrud made very good mousetraps, but he never remembered to clean up the mice afterward.

Planks of wood, bars of copper, and gears stacked in piles and pyramids covered the floor. Dowels stuck out from the plaster of one wall, with ropes, chains, tools, and more gears hanging from them. Clocks hung on the other wall, so many that the wall looked like it was made out of clocks. They all worked, or most of them did—tocking and ticking in rhythms that clashed with each other. It sounded like an argument of clocks.

Scrud bent over his workbench in the middle of the room.

"Jellyweed and impsense!" he shouted at the bench. His voice was cracked and tired. He dropped one twisted tool and picked up another from the wall without clocks. He didn't notice Rownie. There was a gearworked horse's head on the workbench, and this did notice Rownie. The automaton's eyes followed the boy as he picked his way across the floor and tried not to step on anything important.

Rownie took a deep breath. "Hello, Mr. Scrud!" he shouted again. The gearworker scared him, and always had scared him, but Rownie had been here often enough that the fear didn't matter. He felt it, bright and burning, but it didn't stop him from standing in the middle of the floor and shouting Scrud's name.

The gearworker's head snapped up. He looked at Rownie. The gearworked horse looked at Rownie. Then both of them looked away, and Mr. Scrud began to mutter in an undertone. He wasn't shouting. This meant that he was listening.

"Graba paid more than she needed to pay, Mr. Scrud. Last time you fixed her leg, she paid more than she needed to."

"Impsense!" said Scrud. He stuck a long pin in the horse's ear and twisted it. The horse shut one eye.

"It's true, Mr. Scrud," said Rownie. He could see three bottles of gear oil on the shelf behind the workbench. This was what Graba wanted, and Rownie knew that each bottle cost two copper pennies. *Two coppers per audience member, the sign had said. Goblin farce, onstage, for two coppers. Maybe they wear masks. Maybe they juggle fire. Maybe they have metal teeth.*

He was very afraid of what he was about to do. He took another deep breath.

"She overpaid, Mr. Scrud," he said. "She needs two coppers back."

Rownie met Scrud's glare when Scrud stared at him. He would not turn around and run. He showed Scrud that he would not turn around and run by the way he stood there.

Scrud reached up onto the shelf behind him, took down a bottle of gear oil, and put it on the bench where Rownie could reach it.

"No," Rownie said, standing and breathing. "This time she needs the two copper pennies."

The gearworker muttered to himself. He took back the oil, rummaged in his shirt pocket, and put one copper coin on the table. Then he put another on top of it.

Rownie took the coins. "Thank you, Mr. Scrud," he said.

He left the workshop without running. He left the alleyway without running. Behind him the alley filled up with clanking, metallic noises, and shouts. The metal sounded like Graba's bird's legs somewhere behind him. Rownie started running.

* * *

Rownie ran halfway to Market Square, passing familiar fountains and monuments. He stumbled once, caught himself, and paused for breath under the bronze statue of the Mayor. The statue wore a suit with a watch chain tucked into the waistcoat pocket and held out both hands in a way that looked either welcoming or surprised. The metal was old and green-stained, except for the head. The statue got a new head every time the city got a new mayor. Graba had hinted that she would be very pleased if someone stole the Mayor's statue-head and brought it back to her, but so far no one had worked up the courage to try it.

Someone nearby shouted at someone else, and not at Rownie. His insides jumped anyway. He slipped the two coins into the only pocket of his coat, and then he walked and remembered how to breathe as he walked. He wanted to run, but one of the Guard might decide that he was running for Bad Reasons and try to catch him.

Most of Graba's household hated Northside, and got lost in Northside. The streets here followed different rules.

They ran in perfectly straight lines, and met each other at right angles. Rownie knew the landmarks of it, though, and could navigate Northside easily enough.

He passed the Reliquary, and the Northside Rail Station. A member of the Guard stood watch over the station's iron latticework doors. The Guard wore a bright, showy uniform. He held a spear with tassels on it and stared at the opposite side of the street.

Rownie walked by slowly. He wondered why the man was there, guarding a rusted gate. There was only one of him, and if anything crawled up out of the old rail station to break the gate, then one Guard wouldn't do very much good. The Southside Rail Station did not have a Guard posted at the entrance. It did not need one. If anything nasty crawled up from the depths and came to Southside, then Graba would deal with it. Probably. If she wanted to.

Rownie passed the station and came to the square, a huge open space of flagstones with a fountain in the middle and market stalls all around. It was already afternoon, and some of the stalls were closing. A farmer with dozens of long braids pulled down a tent pole, letting the canvas roof of his stall billow and dissolve into a puddle of cloth.

Rownie smelled foods, all kinds. The smells blended

together. They ganged up on him and made it very difficult to think about anything else. He lingered by a baker's stall and smiled. It was his best smile.

The baker passed him some bread. "Yesterday's," she said. "Spoil soon anyway, and there's no one buying."

"Good luck selling tomorrow," Rownie said, or tried to say around the mouthful of dry bread he was crunching on. She passed him another piece for saying so, and waved him away. Then she pulled at a chain behind her. The stall collapsed, folding back into the wall of the square.

Gearwork in the stall squeaked like Graba's right leg. Rownie flinched at the sound.

He dodged around tent poles and covered wagons, moving away from all the bustle to the fountain in the center of the square. A stone bear, a stone lion, and a stone naga all roared streams of water into a cracked stone basin. He cupped water in one hand, slurping up as much as he could. He dipped his other piece of bread in the basin to soften it, but the water only made it soggy.

A pigeon flapped onto the rim of the fountain and looked sideways at Rownie. Sideways is the only way pigeons know how to look. Rownie ignored it. He knew it just wanted some of the bread. He didn't think it was one of Graba's birds. He didn't think so.

Someone grabbed Rownie's arm.

"Give me the bread, Rownie-Runt," said Vass. She had a sack of grain slung over one shoulder. "I'm hungry."

"Let me go," Rownie said. She wouldn't let him go. He gave her the second piece of bread, and she set down the sack to take it, but she still wouldn't let him go.

"Help me carry the chicken feed home," she told him. "The Grubs brought the eggs, but they left me to carry the feed myself. It's heavy." Vass called the rest of the children in Graba's household—the ones without names, the ones who had to make up their own names—"Grubs." She usually said it in a singsong sort of way. *Graba's Grubs, Graba's Grubs.*

"Can't," Rownie said. "I have to do something for Graba."

"Do what?"

"Deliver a message."

"What's the message?"

"I can't tell."

"Then I think you're lying. I think there isn't really any message, so you should help me carry the chicken feed." She put the rest of the bread in her mouth and swung the sack at Rownie. He caught one end to keep it from knocking him over. Vass pushed him, and they started walking south. They walked very slowly south, away from the fairgrounds and away from the goblins.

Vass was twice as tall as he was. She could run much faster than he could. She would catch him if he ran.

They reached the south end of the square. The Guard had already left his post at the rusted station doors, market-time duties done for the day.

Rownie jerked one way, pulling Vass with him, and dropped the sack as he bolted the other way, toward the rusted gate. He pushed against the metal latticework and squeezed through, stumbling in. He felt Vass's hand reach in after him and catch at the edge of his coat. He pulled back.

"Stupid runt!" Vass shouted.

"I have a message from Graba!" Rownie was angry that she wouldn't let him deliver it, even though there wasn't really any message to deliver.

"Stupid," she said. "So stupid. Now the diggers will get you. Can you hear them? Can you hear them behind you?"

Rownie took a step backward, farther in. He didn't look behind him. "It's all flooded," he said. "They dug the tunnel into the River, and now it's all flooded." Everyone knew that. The Mayor wanted to build a railcar track between Northside and Southside. He kept trying, but the tunnel kept flooding.

The Mayor also wanted to tear down the ramshackle

buildings of Southside and replace them with roads that moved in straight lines. That's what Graba always said.

"Folks still hear them digging," Vass told Rownie. "So the diggers are still down there, in the rail tunnel." She let that thought sink in for a while. It sank. Rownie thought about diggers with skin all gray from soaking in River water. He thought about how they would only remember digging, how they would always move forward and break things in front of them with shovels or pickaxes or just their hands. Diggers were people without hearts, without any will of their own, and they just kept doing whatever task they were set to. Rownie wondered if any of them had struck off downward, disoriented by the flood, and if they might pop out the other side of the world someday. He thought about the tunnels behind him, haunted by digging.

"I'll protect you," Vass told him, as sweetly as Vass could say anything. "Come out and carry the sack."

Rownie stepped backward again. "No," he said. Now *he* haunted the tunnels. Now he was something to be afraid of.

Vass spit on the ground. Then she smiled, and it looked like Graba's smile in miniature. "Where's my gear oil, runt?" she asked.

Rownie's heart beat like it wanted to run off without him. "What oil?" Vass had left the house already when

Graba gave him the errand. Vass couldn't have known about it.

"Stop it!" Vass yelled, and Rownie didn't think she was yelling at him. Her eyes were shut. All the muscles of her face were tightly scrunched. "You can't! I'm not a Grub. Stop it, stop it!" Vass stumbled away, out of sight. She took the grain sack with her.

Rownie stood absolutely still. He did not understand what had just happened. He carefully put it on a shelf in the back of his mind, with other things he did not understand.

He listened for shovel sounds and shuffling steps behind him. It was quiet, cold, and heavy in the station, just a few feet from the warm open bustle of the market where Vass might still be hiding, waiting for him.

He stood as long as he could, and then he stood for longer. He did not look behind him. He did not hear shovels or steps or any other sign that the diggers were coming. He finally took three steps of his own and squeezed out through the iron doors.

Vass was gone, and most of the market was gone. A few open wagons rolled away from the empty square. The sky was a darker blue than it had been. Almost dusk. He ran.

Act I, Scene IV

A CLOSED WAGON STOOD IN THE CENTER of the fair-grounds. It had walls and a rooftop, like a small house on wheels. A crowd had gathered beside it. The sky was still blue overhead, but the sun was already gone.

Rownie climbed down the slope from the road to the green. His feet hurt. He heard drums and a flute, though he didn't see any musicians. He made his way to the very back of the crowd. He had to stand off to one side to get a view of the wagon around the thick press of people. He found a spot with a view, and then waited for something to happen. He tried to keep still. He kept shifting his weight.

The wall of the wagon fell over. It stopped level to the ground and became the platform of a stage. Curtains hung where the wall used to be, hiding the space inside the wagon. More curtains dropped around the edge of the platform, hiding the space underneath. Trumpets snapped up from the wagon's roof and played a flourish all by themselves.

A goblin stepped onstage.

Rownie stared. He had never seen one of the Changed before. This one was completely bald, and taller than Rownie thought goblins could get. His sharp ear-tips stuck out sideways from his head, and his eyes were large and flecked with silver and brown. His skin was green; the deep green of thick moss and riverweed. His clothes were patched together from fabric of all different colors.

The goblin bowed. He set two lanterns at both corners of the stage, and then stood in the center. He held several thin clubs in one hand. He watched the audience in a cruel and curious way, the way molekeys watch beetles before they pull off their wings and legs.

Rownie felt like he should be hiding behind something. When the goblin moved, finally, throwing the clubs in the air with a snap of both sleeves, Rownie flinched.

The goblin started to juggle. Then he stomped his foot three times against the platform. A dragon puppet peered out through the curtain behind him. It was made of plaster and paper, and it glowed in golden colors. The puppet breathed fire over the stage. The goblin tossed his clubs up through the dragon breath, and each club caught fire at one end. Then the puppet roared and pulled back through the curtain. The goblin juggled fire.

Rownie tried jumping in place to get a better view. He

wanted to be at the very front of the crowd, at the edge of the stage. He tried to push between knees and shoulders to get there. He couldn't manage it. He clenched his hands and strained forward, but he couldn't force himself to move.

"It will cost you two coppers to be any closer than this," said a voice.

Rownie looked. A small, round, and wrinkled goblin stood beside him.

This one had white hair tied tightly behind her head, and a pair of thick eyeglasses on a little brass chain. She had flecks of gold and bright green in her eyes, which were magnified by the eyeglasses. She held out her hand politely, not too far outstretched. The skin of her hand was a deep green-brown, and her fingers were longer than Rownie thought fingers should be.

Rownie took Graba's pennies from his coat pocket and dropped them in the goblin's hand.

"Thank you," she said, nodding once. "You have paid your way through the audience wall, which is the fifth wall, so you are free to cross it and believe it is not there and only made up of a song and a circle in the grass."

The old goblin moved away. Rownie could hear her voice at the edge of the crowd. "Two coppers if you please, yes?"

He pushed forward, dodging around the knees of many

tall people and working his way to the very front. It was easy enough to do.

The fire juggling ended. The tall goblin extinguished the burning clubs, bowed, and withdrew. A smaller goblin with a trim gray beard and a huge black hat stepped onstage. His face was wide and round, and as he walked, his chin went first in front of him. He leaned on a polished cane, which clacked against the floorboards. He was small—shorter than Rownie—but he moved like he knew himself superior to everyone else gathered there.

"Ladies and gentlemen!" he said. "You have no doubt heard that our profession has been prohibited by his lordship, the Mayor."

Some booed. Others cheered. "We're only here to see you arrested!" someone shouted from the back of the crowd.

The old goblin smiled a polite smile. "I am loath to disappoint my audience, sir, but I believe that I myself, and my companions here, are not so inconvenienced by this law. The citizens of this fair city are prohibited from pretending to be other than they are. We, however, are not citizens. We are not legally considered to be persons. This saddens me, because I lived in this city long before any of you were born, but I will have to quibble with that particular injustice another time. You have come for a play. We will give you a play. We are already Changed—the additional change of a mask and a costume will not do you any harm, and it will not break the law."

Everyone cheered this time—those who wanted to see the show and those who wanted to see goblin actors dragged off by the Guard, who didn't believe that any sort of legal loopholes or flummery would prevent this from happening.

"We will first offer a brief tale to delight the children among you," the goblin said. He took off his hat, and then pulled out the mask of a giant. The mask had a protruding, furrowed forehead and rows of thick, square teeth. Rownie was surprised that the giant mask had fit inside the goblin's hat—though it *was* a very large hat.

The old goblin closed his eyes. Everyone was quiet in that moment, and respectful of that silence—whether or not they wanted to be.

He put on the mask and shifted his stance to tower above them all, even though he wasn't very tall.

"I am a giant," he said in a giant's voice, and it was true because he said that it was true.

Rownie wanted to try it. He wanted to declare himself a giant. He tried to focus on standing still and not bouncing up and down on the balls of his feet.

A slight little goblin came onstage with a whip, a wooden sword, and enormous eyes behind a brave-looking hero mask. The Hero tried to outwit the Giant.

"I've heard that you can change yourself into a lion," said the goblin-hero in a high, crisp voice, "but I don't believe you can manage it."

"Fool," said the goblin-giant in a very deep voice. "I can change into anything I please!" He dropped the giant mask and pulled a lion mask up over his face with one smooth motion. He snarled and crouched.

The audience cheered, but it was a nervous cheer.

"This is not safe," said an old man who stood beside Rownie. His spine was so gnarled and bent over that he had to turn his head sideways to see the stage. "Don't believe it is, just because they're goblins. No masks and no changes, none. Not safe."

"That was wonderful!" said the goblin-hero. "But a magnificent lion is not such a small step away from a giant. Can you change into a python?"

The lion reached into its own mouth and turned the mask inside out. It was a snake now, and it shook slowly from side to side.

"Astonishing!" said the goblin-hero. "But a python is still such a large creature. You cannot have so much magic as to transform yourself into a small and humble housefly."

Metal shutters closed over the stage lanterns. In the sudden dark, Rownie could dimly see the goblin take off his snake mask and toss something in the air.

The lanterns snapped open. A housefly puppet made of paper and gears began to buzz in circles over the stage. The goblin-hero cracked his whip. The housefly exploded in sparks.

"One less giant!" the hero shouted. The crowd clapped. Rownie cheered. "But I wonder if there might be any more?" He peered out into the crowd, and then jumped over the side of the stage. "Any giants over here?" he shouted from somewhere in the dark.

Meanwhile, the old goblin had withdrawn. A gruesome head peered out through the stage curtains, exactly where the dragon puppet had been before. The giant puppet winked at the crowd, one paper eyelid closing over a painted wooden eye.

The puppet spoke. "We must have a volunteer to play our next giant! The mask will fit a child best."

The audience responded with a stunned silence. No one knew if this was a joke. No one knew if it was funny. Everyone knew that even goblinish legal loopholes could never allow an unChanged child to wear a mask.

Rownie expected to hear some sort of official person make an official refusal. He waited for members of the Guard to come forward and forbid any such thing. But there were no members of the Guard nearby. No one said anything at all.

"The child will be perfectly safe!" said the giant puppet. "You there! The tasty-looking one with a hat. Would you like to perform?" It licked its lips with a long puppet tongue, and the crowd finally laughed a nervous laugh. Someone—a father, uncle, or older brother—pulled the child with the hat away from the stage.

The giant puppet searched with its wooden eyes. "You!" it called out. "The one wearing a flower necklace. Play a giant for our story here, and I promise that you will absolutely not spend the next thousand years enslaved in underground caverns. We would never do any such thing."

"No!" the girl shouted back.

"Very well, delectable child." The puppet's eyes moved. "Is there any one among you brave and foolish enough to stand on this stage and impersonate a person of my own great stature?"

Rownie waved his hand in the air. "I'll do it!" He wasn't afraid. He felt like he would be even less afraid if he could stand high up above everyone else. He wanted to command attention, like the old goblin had just done.

The crowd cheered him on, but cruelly, convinced that something awful would certainly happen to him onstage and that they would get to watch it happen. The goblins would take him, and then the Guard would come and take away the goblins. It would be an excellent spectacle to see.

The old man with the bent spine tried to hold Rownie back with one gnarly knuckled hand. "Stupid boy," he said. "Stupid, stupid boy." Other dissenting voices cried out from people unwilling to let a child take such a risk.

Rownie pulled away and tried to climb onto the stage, but he couldn't quite manage it. The stage resisted.

"I offer a compromise!" said the giant puppet. "He may hold the end of an iron chain. The front row of the audience will hold the other end. You can yank him away to safety if the performers here look likely to bite him or curse him or possibly steal him away. Are we agreed? Is this protection enough?"

Some still shouted no, but the rest were louder:

"Let him try it!"

"He'll be fine if he holds iron."

"Stupid kack has it coming if he doesn't!"

Rownie ignored them all. He focused on the giant puppet. The puppet looked down at him. He could see that its eyes were only wood, carved and painted, but he still kept eye contact with it.

"We are agreed," the Giant said, and withdrew behind the curtain.

The goblin with the trim gray beard and the floppy black hat returned to the stage. He took off his hat and drew a length of chain from it. He spread the chain across the front of the stage and nodded to Rownie.

Guess they can *touch iron,* Rownie thought. *Blotches is such a liar.* He took one end of the chain. Other hands took the opposite end.

He pushed forward. He still couldn't climb onto the stage. It wasn't very high, but the air would not move aside for him.

The old goblin reached down. "Give me your other hand," he said in a smaller version of the Giant's booming voice.

Rownie reached up, took the goblin's hand, and scrambled onto the stage. He stood, let go of the hand with the long, green fingers, and held the chain. He faced the curtain, away from the audience. Suddenly he didn't want to turn around and see the crowd looking back at him. He didn't feel set above everyone else, like he'd expected to. He felt at their mercy. He tried to swallow, but his throat was dry.

The old goblin watched him with gold-flecked eyes half closed, considering. "Tell me your name, brave and foolish boy."

"Rownie," said Rownie.

The goblin's already wide eyes widened. "Rownie? A diminutive of Rowan, I believe. How very interesting." He tipped his hat. "A pleasure. My own name is Thomas, and

I have been the first actor of this troupe and of this city since before the walls and towers fell." He picked up the discarded giant mask, setting it on Rownie's shoulders. It was heavy. The paint on it smelled funny.

"Stand there," the goblin whispered, pointing. "I will give you your lines from backstage." He passed through the curtains. Rownie was alone in the center of the platform. He stood where he was supposed to stand, and turned around.

Faces watched him from the dark. Rownie could hear them murmuring and mumbling. He knew from the sound that some were worried, and others delighted, and all of them were sure that something awful was about to happen.

Rownie drew up his shoulders, pushed out his chest, and tried to be very tall. He was a giant. He *was* something awful. *He* was going to happen to somebody else.

The curtain whispered behind him. "What noise was that within my father's house?"

Rownie roared. "What noise was that within my father's house?"

"I smell trespassing blood," the curtain went on. "Now show yourself."

"I smell trespassing blood. Now show yourself!"

The goblin-hero jumped back onto the stage. "Hello!" he said. "I have heard boasting that giants can transform themselves into anything they please. I've come to see if that proud boast is true."

"This truth will be the last you ever learn!" Rownie said, echoing the curtain behind him.

The goblin-hero laughed, but it was a frightened laugh. "It would be worth it. Can someone so tall transform into a small and unChanged boy?"

No lines or instructions came from behind the curtain.

Rownie took off the mask with one hand. He set it on the stage beside him, and then held out his arms as if to say *Look at me!* The chain clinked in his other hand.

"Well done!" the goblin-hero said. "You are small, now, though you still look fierce—"

Rownie grinned. He still felt fierce.

"—but I bet you cannot change into a bird."

The lantern shutters snapped shut. The goblin tossed a paper bird in the air. At that same moment the front row of the crowd, spooked by the sudden darkness, pulled the iron chain and yanked Rownie forward. He tumbled off the edge of the stage.

He felt hands trying to catch him, but he fell through them, hit the ground, and rolled onto his back. He could see the glowing paper bird fly above the dark silhouettes of people standing around him. The bird exploded in sparks, and a cloud of paper feathers drifted down.

"One less giant!" said the goblin-hero from the stage.

Rownie got to his feet. Those around him poked and pinched his arms to make sure he was still there and still real. Then the giant puppet returned, and then roared. It captured their attention. It almost captured Rownie's attention, but he looked away. He didn't want to be reminded that he was outside the story now. He wanted to savor how it had felt to be in the midst of it.

A hand emerged from the red cloth that skirted the bottom of the platform. It waved him closer.

Rownie looked around. No one else had noticed, not even the old man with his neck craned sideways.

The hand waved again. Rownie felt like he was about to jump over the side of the Fiddleway.

He ducked underneath the stage.

Act I, Scene V

IT WAS DARK BENEATH THE STAGE platform. Rownie had to hunch forward like the old man with the bent spine. He turned his head to look around. It didn't help.

A lantern shutter clicked open, but only slightly. Rownie saw gold-flecked eyes staring at him from behind a pair of eyeglasses. "Well done," the goblin, the one to whom he had given two copper coins, whispered. "Yes, it was well done. Do you need something to drink? I find lemon tea soothing after speaking to a crowd."

"Okay," said Rownie. His neck started to hurt. He sat on the ground, so he wouldn't have to hold his head at odd angles anymore. The goblin handed him a wooden mug, lacquer-smooth and filled with hot tea. He smelled it and took a sip. He tasted lemon and honey.

"Tell me your name, yes?" the goblin said.

Rownie glanced at her over the edge of the steaming mug. She was smiling, but he couldn't tell what kind of smile it was. This was strange to him. He always knew exactly how the rest of Graba's household felt, because none of them knew how to hide it. Graba herself never bothered to conceal her moods and wishes—her face was as easily readable as words spelled out in burning oil in the middle of the street. Rownie was used to that. The goblin, however, wrote her smile in a language that Rownie didn't know and couldn't read.

"Rownie," he said.

"Hello, Rownie," she said. "I thought that this might be your name. Mine is Semele. Yes, it is. And I am wondering whether you have heard news of your brother."

Rownie stared at her. He knew what she had asked him, but he didn't understand why she had asked. "My brother Rowan?"

"Yes, Rowan," said Semele. "A decent young actor, that one, and he has been missing for some time. Have you heard from him?"

"No," Rownie said, suspicious. If he *had* heard from his brother, he probably wouldn't tell *anyone* about it—not Graba, and certainly not goblins.

"Well," the goblin said, "please tell him hello if you see him. In the meanwhile, I wonder if you might be interested in remaining with us. We have many performances to make—we play at the Broken Wall tomorrow and down by the docks on the day after that—and we very certainly could use another voice, another pair of hands. Is this something you would like?"

Rownie blinked. Yes, he would like to stand onstage again. Yes, definitely yes. "It might," he said aloud, still suspicious. Living in Graba's household had taught him to be suspicious whenever anyone offered him exactly what he wanted. "Can I watch the rest of the play first?"

"Of course," said Semele.

Rownie finished his tea and set the mug on the ground. Semele pointed to the back of the wagon. Rownie half walked and half crawled underneath the stage. He emerged between the cloth's edge and a wagon wheel.

He could hear a fiddle and a flute from the wagon's roof, and then singing, beautiful singing. He paused to listen, and he wondered what to do.

He did not actually get to decide. Metal shrieked against metal. Wood and brass talons closed around him from behind.

"Where is my gear oil, runt?" Graba hissed in Rownie's ear.

She lifted him up with a bird's leg as though he weighed less than dust or a name or a crumpled scrap of paper. Then she wrapped her arm around his waist and set off with long strides.

Rownie squirmed. Graba held him close and sniffed.

"You smell wrong," Graba said. "You smell like thieving and tin. You smell unsettled. Did Semele brew you Change potions?"

"No, Graba," he tried to say, but he couldn't actually say it. She held him tight, and his breath came out in short gasps.

Graba strode across the green and onto the roadway, moving fast. Rownie thought furiously about different ways he might escape or explain himself. He thought and thought and came up with nothing and more nothing.

They passed beneath the statue of the Lord Mayor. Graba spat at his feet. They crossed the Fiddleway and passed beneath the Clock Tower. Graba spat at the foot of the tower.

Graba strode into Southside. They passed through an open lot of hard-packed dirt and broken plaster walls. It was a place where old buildings had fallen over, and new ones had not yet come and might never come. Night birds pecked in the dirt. Two peacocks slept on the top of a brick chimney that stood alone, without walls.

"This was home, a long while ago," Graba said as they went through. "This was mine. Every place I put down my shack is mine, though none of them ever own me."

Rownie said nothing. Breathing was all he could do.

Graba stopped, finally, outside her own shack. Vass and

Stubble peeked out through the window that served as their only door. Rownie expected his older siblings to look smug. He expected them to gloat. Someone was in trouble, and it wasn't either one of them.

They didn't look smug. They didn't gloat. They looked afraid.

Until this moment Rownie had been startled, surprised, and scared of what might happen next. Now he felt fear, bone-deep inside him. Now he knew that Graba was upset over worse than the loss of two pennies.

Graba would never fit through the small window-door. She climbed up the sides of the alleyway instead, one long leg stretched out to either wall. She hoisted them both onto the roof, and then lifted half of the shingled rooftop like a box's lid. She climbed inside and tossed Rownie into the far corner of her loft. The rooftop fell shut above them. Birds shrieked and flapped their wings. Graba settled onto her stool. She watched Rownie with pale eyes. "Did you eat what she gave you?" she whispered. "Did you drink what she offered?"

Rownie stared back at her and said nothing. He needed to know what kind of trouble he was in, and he didn't know.

"I can burn you," Graba said. It was almost kind, the way she said it. "I can burn goblin gifts out of you, now. I should do that, before you start to Change into one of them, just as she did. I should burn away whatever she gave you." She lit the iron stove, took a mortar and pestle down from a high shelf, and began to pound dried leaves into a fine powder. She chanted softly to herself. She never took her eyes away from Rownie, and Rownie never took his eyes away from her. The only light in the room came from the door of the stove.

Graba set the mortar down. She took a handful of the powder in one hand and a pigeon from the rafters in the other. The pigeon held on to one of Graba's fingers with delicate bird's feet. She sang to it, a low song, and then sprinkled the powder over it. The bird caught fire in her hand. It shrieked. Its feathers smelled sharp and bitter as they burned.

Graba held the fire between herself and Rownie. She watched Rownie through it. She chanted, and the song in her voice made her words stronger, stickier, and more a part of the world of solid things. "By voice and by fire. By blood and by fire. My home will not know you. My home knows no Changelings. Fire will send you, and Rowan replace you. Too old for the Changing was mask-wearing Rowan."

She leaned in closer, chanting. "If you came from the grave hearth, return to the grave hearth. If you came from the River, may floodwaters take you. If you came from hill demons, are of the hill demons, go back to the doorways set into their hills. I call banishment on you from every direction!"

"Graba?" Rownie said, and tried to think of something more to say, something that would make her merely annoyed with him.

Graba's talon caught him and held him up, squirming by the scruff of his coat. She brought him closer to the flames in her hand. She kept her eyes fixed on Rownie's face as she chanted. Her chanting voice took on a snarl.

"Semele will not Change you. Her charms will run howling, her words lose their making, her songs lose their binding. What she hides will be found, what she shows will be hidden. She will not take from me. Her works will be scalded." Fire flared up from her palm. Rownie felt it singe away the fine hairs on his face.

He stopped struggling, closed his eyes, and reached for the crank in Graba's shin. He popped it out of place and sent it spinning the wrong way around. Springs lost their tension inside Graba's leg, and she dropped Rownie at the windowsill.

The window was open. Rownie jumped. He didn't have time to look first. His foot caught on the sill, and it twisted him around. He fell backward, and then down.

Graba threw the burning bird down after him. The greasy fireball stood bright against the sky. Rownie watched it while he fell.

Act I, Scene VI

ROWNIE LANDED IN A SLOPING PILE of dust, and slid down. A dustfish flopped into his hair, flopped out again, and wriggled away to go about its dusty business. Fire, bad-smelling and bird-shaped, smacked against the pile beside him. It smoldered and sizzled there.

Rownie lay still, gasping. He thought very hard about getting up, getting somewhere safely away from the burning bird and away from Graba's rage. He thought about it, but he did not actually move. The landing had knocked the breath out of him, and he was not yet sure how to get it back.

He looked up, expecting to see another burning bird, or a live and larger bird come to peck his eyes out of his face—or else Graba's other talon, still wound-up and able to reach through the window and grasp at him. He saw none of these things, so he lay still and tried to figure out if he had broken anything. His arms and legs and head were all sore from the landing, but nothing was bleeding, and none of his bones seemed to have snapped. Rownie experimented with moving his legs and found out that he still could. He slowly got to his feet.

Stubble climbed through the first-floor window. He stared at Rownie. He had a broken broomstick in his hand. He looked shocked, and still afraid, but he held the stick just like he always did when he played the King of All Pirates. Blotches and Greasy climbed through the window behind him.

Rownie might have been the smallest and the youngest in all of Graba's household, but he was not the most recent one to join them. He remembered when Greasy first stood before Graba, up in the loft. She had marked his face with ash and spit. She had marked him as belonging to her. Rownie didn't know where Greasy had come from. Maybe he was just another dustchild of Southside, with nowhere else to be and a liking for the thuggish swagger that came with joining Graba's household and running Graba's errands. Maybe Graba had made him out of birds—probably pigeons, in his case. Pigeons were greasy.

The burning pigeon blackened into a greasy smear at Rownie's feet.

Stubble advanced, and then hefted his broomstick, but Rownie was no longer willing to be smacked with rusty swords on the backs of his knees, or anywhere else. He had changed roles. Stubble was very much taller, but Rownie was a giant. He stood like a giant. He walked directly up to Stubble and took the stick away from him, just as a giant would.

"Thanks," he said, as though the older boy had been offering it to him rather than threatening him with it.

Stubble looked lost. He looked like he no longer knew what kind of story he was in. But then his expression changed. It took on some of Graba, with one eye squinty and the other eye wide. He watched Rownie with Graba's look, with a piece of Graba inside his head, and the look she gave was angry.

Greasy and Blotches each took on a little of Graba's expression.

Others climbed out through the window, Lanks and Bilk and Filtch and Jabber and Mot. They were all of them Grubs, and all of them looked at Rownie with Graba's stare and squint.

Rownie was no longer a giant. He turned away and ran as fast as he could force his legs to run.

He heard many footsteps smack against the dirt and dusty cobblestones behind him. He dropped the broken broomstick. He couldn't possibly fend off a whole gaggle of Grubs with a stick, and it got in the way of his running.

Rownie dodged from one cramped and narrow lane into another. He took sudden corners and curving streets. He followed the wild and roundabout logic of Southside, and he navigated by memory almost as much as by moonlight. It would have been easier to see on the wider roads, with their rare lantern lights burning above important intersections, but Rownie was more afraid of being seen than he was of tripping over something he couldn't see. He needed to disappear. He kept to the small and unlit roads.

Guzzards squawked at him from rubbish piles in the dark. They were ornery things, large and flightless trash-picking birds, and Rownie tried to keep his distance from their squawking.

He couldn't disappear. The Grubs were too close behind him. They ran in silence. Rownie had never known them to keep quiet, not ever, not even while sleeping.

He stumbled his way through a thick drift of dust, coughed when it peppered the back of his throat, and kept running. It felt as though he had always been running. His legs and his lungs ached. He didn't remember what it was like to be still.

Footsteps sounded close behind him. He couldn't out-run them. He needed to hide.

Rownie dodged left, onto a wide open street, and ran for the rusted gate of the Southside Rail Station.

At that moment he was far more afraid of Grubs than of diggers or ghouls or whatever else might be waiting for him in the station—as long as the diggers and ghouls did not look at him with Graba's look and all of Graba's anger.

Maybe the others would be afraid of ghouls. Maybe they wouldn't follow him inside.

He reached the gate and squeezed through the bars. He held the end of his coat with one hand, to keep it from catching on the gate—and to keep Grubs from catching it as it trailed behind him.

For the first time since he started running, Rownie paused.

The others were not small enough to follow him through the bars. They reached the gate, and then began to climb. They did not taunt him. They did not insult him. They did not say anything at all.

Rownie ran from that silence. He pushed himself forward, through the dark of the Southside Rail Station.

* * *

The station was a vast, open space. Rownie could tell by the way sound moved through it. His feet smacked the polished stone floor. The sound went out away from him, echoed, and got lost somewhere in the open space. He tried to move quietly, but his feet still smacked against stone.

There was a tiny bit of light. The ceiling was glass,

and moonlight shone dimly through its smudged surface. It made the ceiling visible, high overhead, but it did not illuminate very much beneath. Dark shapes loomed around Rownie, and he tried to avoid them.

He moved as quickly as he dared, with both arms groping in front of him. He hoped to find obstacles with his hands before he found them with his face. He found one with his shin instead. It was metal. The pain in his leg made lights flash inside his eyes. He shut them. He also shut his mouth. He didn't cry out. He wouldn't cry out.

Rownie felt with his hands to see what he had run into. It was a bench made out of wrought iron, curved and stylish, for important people to sit on while they waited for the railcar to take them to Northside. He crawled underneath it. It was big enough to hide him, and to keep anyone else from bumping into him in the dark.

He waited. He couldn't hear anything except his own heartbeat and his own breathing, and he tried very hard to silence both of those things. He was sure the Grubs would be able to hear his pounding heartbeat from all the way across the station floor.

The floor was cold. It felt cold under his hands. It smelled cold, and dusty.

Rownie tried not to think about all of the possible things that might haunt the station around him. He tried not to think about diggers, especially drowned diggers, crawling up from the flooded tunnel. He tried not to think about ghouls. He tried not to think about the gearworkers who used to be sane, who used to make sense when they spoke, before the Lord Mayor of Zombay gathered them all together to make grand and glorious projects like rail stations. Now the gearworkers were all as cracked as Mr. Scrud, and nothing they said ever made sense. Rownie tried not to wonder what it was that cracked them all, and he tried not to imagine that it was still here, somewhere in the station. He tried not to imagine that he could hear it breathing. He was fairly certain that he could hear *something* breathing, something big, somewhere in the dark.

Many pairs of bare feet smacked the stone. The sound echoed all around him.

"Rownie-Runt!" Blotches called. It was Blotches's voice, but the syllables sounded like Graba.

"Stop your hiding, now," called Greasy. He spoke like Graba.

"I'll be so much less angry if you come out," called Stubble, his voice rising and falling the way Graba's voice rose and fell. "I've got things to ask of you."

"Come out, you Changeling thing!" Blotches shouted, his voice rusty and furious.

Rownie stayed where he was, as still as he could manage. He stopped wondering about what else might haunt the station. It was haunted by Grubs, and he didn't think that there could be anything worse. He focused on breathing silently. He got ready to run, if he needed to run.

Someone passed near Rownie's bench. Rownie heard him muttering. It sounded like it might be Greasy. Rownie hoped so. Greasy wasn't very fast. Whoever it was moved off again.

Rownie heard pigeon wings overhead. He peered out from underneath the bench to see dark, feathered shapes pass beneath the faint glow of the ceiling. They circled. They searched.

"Vass, are you here?" Stubble asked loudly, still in Graba's voice. "Make light for me now."

Rownie heard Vass chanting, somewhere in the dark, and then it wasn't dark anymore. Light bloomed and blinded him.

Large clocks hung from the ceiling by great lengths of chain, like the pocket watches of giants. Each clock was also a lantern, and now every lantern burned. They swayed slowly back and forth as pigeons landed on them and pushed off again. The light that they cast made long and swaying shadows.

Rownie watched the Grubs from underneath his iron bench. He watched them search for him in the rows of railcars. The mirrored, brass finish of the cars looked tarnished and old, even though they had never been used.

He waited until he was sure that no one looked in his direction, and then he crawled away from the bench and into the shadow of a stone pillar. He crept carefully down the length of the shadow, farther into the station.

The whole place looked like Northside, with its polished stone and precise angles. It was strange to be south of the River, but seem to be in Northside. Rownie tried not to let it bother him, because he had worse things to be bothered about, and quirks of architecture were down among the very least of his concerns—but he still found it distracting and disorienting. There was a logic to moving through Southside, and that logic no longer worked inside the rail station. Rownie had to make a gear shift in his head, and in his movements, to make sense of his surroundings and to find somewhere to hide. He had to pretend he was north of the River.

Stubble called to him, somewhere very close by. Rownie's insides jumped at the noise. He couldn't tell where it was coming from. He climbed up inside one of the railcars to get quickly out of sight.

Rows of chairs filled the inside of the car. The chairs looked soft and comfortable. They were made out of polished wood, and had faded red cushions. Small, round tables stood between some of the chairs, with streaks of green patina across their copper surfaces. A few lanterns burned on the walls to either side, lit by Vass's chant.

Rownie knew that Vass had a little talent for curses and charms—or at least he knew that she bragged about it— but he had never seen her do anything so grand before. He had also never seen a sibling look at him with Graba's look, or speak with the rhythms of Graba's voice, before Vass did so in the Market Square. *She can wear us like masks*, Rownie thought, and he wondered if it was something Graba might do to him. He started to panic at the thought. The weight of everything he didn't know about his own home pressed down on him and squeezed like Graba's talon-toes. He did not feel like a giant. He felt like the furthest thing from a giant. A bug, maybe. A burnbug or a beetle.

Graba can't wear me, he decided. *She can't. She won't. She wouldn't have to send everyone else to look for me, if she could.*

He moved carefully down the railcar's center aisle. He felt trapped inside the car, and he knew that he shouldn't stay. The others were already searching railcars, one by one. They would find him if he stayed. Rownie didn't know what would happen then. He didn't want to know.

He glanced up at the far entrance. Vass stood there, watching him.

Act I, Scene VII

ROWNIE TOOK IN A LONG BREATH, and let it out. He stood up. He did not run. She would catch him if he ran. He showed her that he would not run by the way that he stood there, and he waited to see what would happen next.

Vass continued to watch him. She smiled her cruel smile, and otherwise she did not move.

"Do you see him, now?" asked Stubble from outside the car. "Have you found him?"

Vass looked directly at Rownie. "No, Graba," she said. "He isn't here."

"Be sure about it," said Stubble. "And bring me back a mirror if you can find an unbroken one, and also a new cushion for my chair."

"Yes, Graba," said Vass. "I think the runt might have ducked into the tunnel. It's not as flooded down there as it should be."

"Seven curses on the several chins of the Lord Mayor,"

said Stubble. "He's pumping the water out of it again. I can hear the breathing and the clanking of his siphons, making it dry. I will go looking there."

"Yes, Graba," said Vass.

She went to sit at one of the copper tables, crossed her legs, and folded her hands in front of her. She wasn't so much taller than Rownie while sitting.

Rownie sat in the chair across from her. "Thank you," he whispered, and he meant it—but he also meant it as a question. He couldn't remember a single time that Vass had helped him with anything, and this seemed like an unlikely moment for her to start. It was no small thing to lie to Graba.

Vass waved his thanks away with one hand. "She treated me like a Grub today. She can't do that. I won't let her do that, not to me. She wears them. She uses them to go places. She's always moving, always, even when she's still at home and upstairs. But I won't let her wear me. I'm not a Grub."

"Me neither," said Rownie, and he hoped it was true. "I've got a name."

Vass smiled her cruel smile. "No, you don't," she said. "You just have Rowan's name, made small. But Graba can't wear you."

Rownie very much hoped that she wasn't lying. "Why not?"

"Because you've got a little talent for wearing masks," Vass said. "Why do you think she keeps you around?" She took a cushion from the chair beside her, looked it over, and knocked some of the dust out by whacking it against the table.

Rownie tried to blink the dust cloud out of his eyes. "Why would masks matter to Graba?"

"Forget it," said Vass. "What matters to Graba shouldn't much matter to you, not anymore. I'm going to douse the lights. We'll leave then. We'll stop looking for you, once it's dark."

"Thanks for helping me hide," Rownie said.

Vass shook her head, forcefully, like there was something stuck to her nose and she wanted it off. "Don't thank me," she said. "I'm not helping you. I'm not doing this for you." She stood up, still holding the cushion. "Wherever you go after tonight," she said, "wherever you end up, just make sure to keep away from the riverbank. The River's angry. The floods are coming."

The floods are coming. The floods were always coming, but Rownie couldn't remember a time when they actually came. It was just something people said—though there was a difference to the way Vass said it, as though the floods were coming soon.

Rownie wanted to ask what she meant, but Vass was no longer paying attention to him. Her eyes lost their focus and looked somewhere else.

"My charm is now ended," she chanted softly. "The knots are untied." Rownie felt the air change around them. He felt the world change shape to her words.

The lights went out. Rownie heard Vass leave the railcar in the dark.

Various Grubs shouted their protests outside. They spoke like Grubs now, and not like Graba.

"You're a kack at the witchwork," said Blotches. "Shouldn't get to keep your name."

"I'm still learning," Vass answered him, sullen. "And I can't keep anything lit for long without oil to burn. Maybe we should stick a wick in Greasy and use *him* for a lantern."

"Shut it," said Greasy.

"The runt probably doubled back and left already," Vass said, "or else he went down the tunnel, and the diggers got him."

"There aren't *really* any diggers in the tunnel," said Greasy. "Are there?"

"Oh yes," said Vass. "Of course there are. Want to see? Should we toss you down there?"

"Shut it!" said Greasy.

The noise of their voices faded as they found their way out of the Southside Rail Station.

Rownie was left alone.

Act I, Scene VIII

ROWNIE TRIED TO SUMMON up the feeling that *he* was haunting the Southside Rail Station, and that other sorts of haunting things should be afraid of *him*—but he couldn't quite convince himself that this was true. He felt sure and certain that there were diggers in the tunnel. He felt unsure and uncertain about what Vass had told him.

Graba can't wear you—you've got a little talent for wearing masks.

Rowan had been very good with masks. He had been wearing one the last time Rownie had seen him, the last time anyone had seen him. That had been months ago, in a Southside alehouse.

* * *

"This is just a little alehouse show," Rowan said. "We'll stand on tables in the back. Maybe the crowd will listen to us while they eat their supper. Maybe they won't."

"Bet the Guard'll come," said Greasy. "They've been

taking actors away. They make 'em into diggers."

Rowan smiled, and shook his head. "We're in South-side," he said. "Since when does Southside pay much attention to the sillier edicts of our good Lord Mayor? Don't worry about it."

"Just don't wear a mask of Graba," said Vass. "She hates the thought that anyone might ever take her place."

"You imitate Graba's voice all the time," Rowan reminded her. He switched into a Graba-voice of his own. "Run some errands for me, child. Go fetch me the sun and the moon and the stars by suppertime. Do that for me, now."

Rownie laughed, and Rowan laughed. It felt like the same laugh.

Vass didn't laugh. Her forehead creased. "Masks are different," she said.

"Do you get to wear any big, scowly pirate masks?" Rownie asked his older brother.

"Looks like you're wearing one already," Rowan told him. He reached down and poked Rownie's real nose with the tip of one finger. "Nice mask, there."

"Yours is even scowlier," Rownie said, and then the two of them tried to top each other for the best scowly face until it was time for the show to start.

"Here," said Rowan. "Hold my coat until the play is done." He gave Rownie his dust-colored overcoat, and then ducked behind a curtain made of two sheets and a broom-stick.

The characters in the play didn't have proper names. The hero was called Youth, and he went on adventures and kept trying to do heroic things. Rowan, behind a bearded, grinning mask, played Youth's best friend, Vice. He carried a broken sword, pulled pennies out of other actors' ears with a quick sleight of hand, and used the pennies to buy wine. He kept trying to get Youth to drink his wine.

Once, Rowan looked out into the audience, caught Rownie's eye, and winked behind the Vice mask.

"He'll get arrested," said Greasy. "They'll take him away and torture him, and *then* they'll make him into a digger."

"Shut it," said Vass. "I'm trying to listen."

"They will not. They will not." Rownie whispered twice. But it was right at that moment that the Guard marched through the door.

The alehouse became very quiet. Everyone put down their mugs and their plates.

The captain of the Guard stepped onto a stool, and then onto a table. The patrons whose table it was quickly moved their food out of his way. The Captain unrolled a parchment, cleared his throat, and read from it.

"It is not lawful to wear masks in Zombay. A barge sailor has learned his skill and craft, but an actor may wear a mask and mimic his manner without any such skills. If the actor tried to steer a barge, he would run it aground."

The actors laughed. "Probably," one of them said.

"A Guard has earned the right to wear a sword," the Captain continued, "through service and sacrifice. An actor cheapens that right by wearing a mask and swinging swords for show."

No one laughed. One of the actors was playing a Guard. Wide wooden gears protruded from the actor's mask where the eyes should be. The small glass gears of the Captain's eyes rotated in short, ticking increments as he read.

"It is a great honor to be an alderman. An actor can siphon away this honor by wearing masks and robes to mimic the outward show of their office. Therefore, by order of the Lord Mayor of all Zombay, the business of plays will cease. Players are liars. Citizens may not be players and must not pretend to be other than they are."

The rest of the Guard arrested each actor and led them away from the makeshift stage. Rowan still wore his mask, and the mask was grinning. Rownie couldn't see what his brother's face was doing underneath.

They marched Rowan to the door beneath the ticking glare of the Guard Captain, who still stood on the table. Rowan's mask grinned up at the Captain. Then Rowan kicked one of the table legs. It broke. The Guard

Captain fell forward with a clang and a crash.

Rowan jumped aside, dodged around flailing arms, and disappeared into the back rooms, where the kitchens were. Rownie could hear broken plates and angry yells after two of the Guard followed Rowan. The Captain got to his feet and shouted in his very loud voice. One of his copper boots was dented, and the foot stuck out at an odd angle.

"We'd better go," said Greasy.

"Obviously," said Vass.

Rownie stared at the kitchen doorway. He wanted to follow his brother. He wanted to know for sure and certain that Rowan had gotten safely away. But too much had happened, too quickly, and now the commotion was already over. He held Rowan's coat tightly to him while he followed Vass and Greasy. They all slunk out and away from the alehouse.

Rownie had hoped that his brother would be waiting for them at Graba's shack, even though he was too old and too tall to still sleep there. He couldn't bunk with the rest of his troupe, not now that everyone had been arrested, and the shack would be a very good place to hide him from the Guard. The Guard always kept clear of Graba. But Rowan didn't show up to hide in the shack. Days and weeks went by without any word.

He's still hiding, Rownie told himself, over and again.

Maybe he sailed away downstream to get clear of the Guard. But he'll come back, and then we'll sail away together and fight pirates, or else we'll be pirates. He'll come back.

Rownie wondered how his brother would find him now that he had run away from Graba's household and was curled up in an abandoned railcar and listening for diggers in the tunnel.

He tried to remember the giant mask on his shoulders. He tried to imagine himself as a giant, towering and untouchable. He also tried to imagine himself Rowan-like, moving easily through the world and laughing along with everything in it. He wrapped Rowan's coat more tightly around himself and curled up on the cushioned railcar seat. He felt very small.

Sleep was impossible. Then the rushing excitement of running and hiding drained away from him and left exhaustion behind. Somehow he slept.

He dreamed that Rowan still wore the vice mask he had been wearing at the alehouse. The mask grinned. That was what it did best.

Dream Rowan reached up and turned the mask inside out. It became a mask of Graba, with one eye squinting and the other eye wide. Then it *was* Graba who stood there, and no longer Rowan. She perched on the edge of the goblin stage. She reached behind her with one bird's foot, a *real* bird's foot covered with black and purple scales, like a guzzard's. She pulled back the curtain. Behind the curtain was the River. It flooded through and covered the stage and covered the city.

Rownie woke up. He felt the cushioned chair underneath him, expecting to find the straw floor of Graba's shack. He didn't, and he didn't know why—not until he gathered up all the pieces of yesterday and put them back together in his head. Then he remembered how alone he was.

Sunlight peered down through the tarnished glass of the arched ceiling, outside the railcar. It was morning. Pigeons roosted on the tops of the hanging clocks. They seemed to be ignoring him. He didn't think they were Graba's birds. He didn't think so.

He crept out of the station and slipped through the bars of the rusted gate. A few scattered people were going about their morning business. He picked a direction and started walking.

Zombay was a different place to him now, and for the first time in his life Rownie felt lost in it.

ACT II

Act II, Scene I

ROWNIE WAS HUNGRY. This was usually true. Hunger was a constant background noise buzzing in the back of his head and the bottom of his stomach. But yesterday he had spent more effort than usual, running toward goblins and away from Grubs, and now he needed some of it back.

He let his legs take him in search of food. He found some outside the tin-roofed house of Mary Mullusk, a pale woman who thought that her family was trying to poison her. She rarely took more than one bite of anything before she threw it out her window. Rownie got there just in time to catch a green apple as it came sailing across the street.

"I wouldn't eat that," Miss Mullusk called to him. She sounded calm for someone who believed herself surrounded by poisoners. "It's a tainted thing."

Rownie bit into the apple, smiled, and shrugged. It tasted fine. It tasted perfect. She shook her head and left the window. He waited to see if she would toss away any other tainted things, but she didn't.

It started to rain. Rownie tightened his coat and breathed in rain smells of dusty mud and wet stone. He tried to clear his head. He was still tired and still alone. It was worse than how he felt on days when Graba moved her shack without warning anyone first or telling them where she intended to go. Rownie knew where the shack was this time, but he couldn't go back there. It was no longer home.

He missed Rowan. But he didn't know where Rowan might be, and he didn't know where to start looking.

The heavy rain faded to a drizzle. Each misty droplet seemed to hang perfectly still, as though someone had shouted "Stop!" at the rain, and the rain had listened. Rownie moved through the hovering drops.

He decided to start with the alehouse in Broken Wall, where he had last seen his brother, to find out if anyone there knew anything at all. This was what you were supposed to do when you lost something—go to the last place you remembered seeing it, even if it had been a couple of months ago. He also had another reason to find the alehouse. *We play at the Broken Wall tomorrow*, the old goblin had said. She had offered him welcome. Rownie could be a part of the goblin troupe. He could be a giant again. He could help them put on plays. Or he could slave away for thousands of years in goblinish underground cities, if that's what they *really* wanted him for.

Broken Wall was the name of the alehouse, and also the name of the neighborhood. It was a part of Southside where most of the buildings had been pieced together with stone from the old city wall—or else carved *into* the larger, solid blocks of the old city wall. It was a long walk to get there, and it took Rownie most of the day. He didn't hurry. He didn't run. His legs were still sore, and he had only scrounged up a single apple. Hunger was still there, buzzing in the middle of him.

When he got to the alehouse, he found goblins in the outside yard. Thomas stood on the roof of their wagon. He was shouting and waving his big black hat.

"I will write you into our next play!" Thomas roared. "I will sculpt your face into grotesque caricatures and paste them onto small, ugly puppets!" The alehouse windows and doors were all shut. No one seemed to be listening to the old goblin, but he continued to roar invective at the walls. "I'll pen your name into immortal verse, and for a thousand years it will be synonymous with ridicule and scorn!"

Rownie stood at the corner of the building and wondered what the fuss was about. He was glad to see a familiar face—even one with a long nose and pointy ears—but he didn't want to stand between a cursing goblin and the object of his ire. He didn't want one of the curses to fly off course and hit him by accident.

"Excuse me," said someone behind him.

He moved out of the way. A small, slight goblin passed him with two arms full of costumes. She wore the sort of dress a lady might wear, but with the skirts hitched up over her shoulder and a soldier costume visible underneath. Her short hair was rain-wet and spiky.

A mask fell from the top of the costume pile as she went by. Rownie caught it before it hit the ground. The mask was feathered, and it sported a long, curved beak. It looked unsettling. Rownie held it so that the empty eyes weren't looking up at him, and he followed the walking pile of costumes.

"You dropped this," he started to say, but the goblin didn't hear him. She was already shouting up at Thomas.

"Haven't we put enough of our enemies into immortal verse already?" she asked. "Do we really need to humiliate a stupid alewife and her very stupid husband for the next thousand years? Really? We've already named villains after the players who stole Semele's script book, and that farmer who set his dogs after us, and the alderman with the funny nose. I can't remember what he did to deserve it. What did that alderman do to deserve an eternity of scorn?"

Thomas ignored her. He may not have heard her. "I will curse this place!" he shouted. "Your ale will turn! Your bread will be maggot-ridden! I will visit humiliations upon you in verse!"

The small goblin climbed the stairs at the back of the wagon, pushed open a door with her foot, and went inside. The door shut behind her.

Rownie knocked on the door. "You dropped this," he said to the door, but it didn't open.

"May the River take you!" Thomas raged above. "May the floods take your household and drown your bones! I will have our artificer build a pair of gearworked ravens, and they will croak your vile name outside your bedroom window, every night, at irregular intervals! You will never sleep again!" He lowered his voice then, but only a little. "Does anyone remember his name?"

"Cob," said someone else. "My father's name is Cob."

It was a young-sounding voice. Rownie looked around the side of the wagon to see who it belonged to.

A dark-haired girl stood in one of the alehouse doorways. She carried a basket in front of her.

Thomas climbed down from the wagon roof and stood before the girl. The rain picked up, and water poured down all sides of his hat.

"Cob," he repeated. "That is an easy syllable for a

gearworked raven to remember and croak at him. What brings you out in the rain, Cob's daughter?"

"I'm just sorry he tossed you out," the girl said. "You should have some payment for the show, so I brought you some bread." She lifted the basket she held. "It's fresh. It doesn't have maggots in it, not unless your curses work very fast." She gave him the basket.

"I withdraw my curses on your household," the old goblin said. He hummed a tune, making his words into a song and a charm, stronger than just a saying. "I may yet carve a grotesque mask in your father's likeness, but I withdraw each curse. May the flood pass your doorstep and leave dry your boots."

"Thank you," the girl said. "The dancers were all perfect. Please tell them."

"I will," he said. "But to whom should I attribute this critique? I have not yet caught your name, young lady."

"I'm Kaile," she said.

Thomas took off his hat and bowed. "Thank you, Kaile, for the tribute of your compliments and the bounty of your family's bakery." Then he rummaged around in his hat and produced a small, gray flute. "This token is yours, I think."

Kaile took the flute. Then someone bellowed at her from the alehouse door, and the girl hurried back inside. The door slammed behind her.

Thomas seemed to diminish where he stood. He returned to the wagon with his head down, and almost bumped hat-first into Rownie.

Rownie meant to say something like, *Excuse me, sir, but one of the other players dropped this. I saved it from getting very muddy and probably stepped on.* Instead he just said, "Here," and handed over the bird mask.

The goblin took it from him and dropped it in the basket with the bread. "Much obliged," he said gruffly. He did not sound obliged, not even a little. He sounded disgruntled and tired. Then he looked more closely at Rownie. "I know you," he said. "You played a giant for us, and not badly—but you vanished afterward."

"Sorry," Rownie said. "My grandmother was angry."

"I see," said Thomas. "Well, would you consider . . ." The goblin paused. Then he shoved Rownie underneath the wagon.

Rownie slipped in the mud and slid to a stop. He was not happy about being shoved. He almost shouted something about that unhappiness. Then he heard Guard-boots marching, and saw the boots stand between the wagon and the road. Rownie decided it would be better to be quiet.

One pair of boots stepped forward.

"I have heard noise complaints," the Captain announced. Rownie knew his voice. He remembered his voice from the alehouse, from the proclamation he gave while standing on a table. "Have you heard anything about a raving goblin throwing curses?"

"I have not," Thomas said, "though I am impressed that the Captain of the Guard himself investigates such a minor concern. Your attention to even the most trivial duties is commendable, and I am very glad to see you. The proprietors of this alehouse have stiffed us payment for performing here, and I wish to register my own complaint."

"Noted," said the Captain, though he did not sound like he had actually taken note. "I am also given to understand that goblins put a mask on an unChanged child yesterday, in front of a crowd of witnesses. Goblins have masked an unChanged citizen of Zombay."

"That would be a terrible thing," Thomas said, gravely and seriously. "I am deeply stricken that anyone would think simple Tamlin performers, such as ourselves, could be capable of such an irresponsible deed."

The Captain took a step forward. Rownie shuffled back a bit, underneath the wagon.

"The Lord Mayor would be very interested in the whereabouts of *any* unChanged actor," the Captain said. "Even a child, even someone who has only worn a mask once. In exchange for such information, the Lord Mayor could provide you with a special license to perform within the proper limits of the city."

"That is very generous," said Thomas. "Very generous. We would, of course, be delighted to help the Lord Mayor with his interests."

Rownie braced himself for more running. He knew how to get away from the Guard. He knew how to zig and zag in Southside streets and escape from those who only ever marched in straight lines. His legs hated the thought of running again, but he braced himself anyway. He would run if he had to. He would make himself run.

Thomas went on. "If we hear the slightest rumors about unChanged actors, we will of course find you immediately."

Rownie took a breath. He had been holding it. He hadn't noticed. He wouldn't have to run. The old goblin wasn't about to turn him in.

"Do so," said the Captain. "I have further business here, but my officers will happily escort you to a proscribed area at this time."

"Certainly, sir," said Thomas, with politeness and courtesy. "Certainly."

The Guard-boots made precise turns, and surrounded them. Rownie heard Thomas climb up into the driving seat. A gearworked mule unfolded itself at the front of the wagon. Rownie could see coal glowing red in its belly.

They use coal, he thought, horrified.

The mule began to trot. Rownie's hiding place was moving, and now he had nowhere to go. There were Guardboots in every direction he looked.

A hatch opened in the wagon floor above him. Several pairs of hands reached down, caught him, and pulled him inside.

Act II, Scene II

GEARWORKS CLANKED. Wooden wheels clacked. The wagon lurched forward, and the hatch in the floor fell shut. Rownie rolled away from the hatch and the grasping hands. They let go of him.

He looked up. The first thing he saw was the dragon.

The fire-breathing puppet hung down from ropes tied to the ceiling, and it pitched as the wagon moved along uneven streets. The wheels went over a bump, and the dragon lurched down at Rownie, as though trying to bite his face. Lantern light glinted on sharp, brass teeth.

He knew it was a puppet. He could see that most of it was plaster and paper on a wooden frame. But he couldn't help flattening himself against the floor and throwing up his arms around his face.

He lowered his hands when nothing happened. The dragon puppet swayed above him. That was all it did.

Four goblins also stood above him.

One was the tall, bald goblin who had juggled fire. He looked at Rownie like he couldn't quite decide what Rownie was. Another wore rough clothes stained with grease and sawdust. She had long, dark hair pulled behind her head and tied with a string—though most of it had escaped the string. The third was the one who had carried a pile of costumes through the rain a few moments ago, and wore more than one set of costumes herself. She had spiky hair. She gave a little wave with one hand.

The fourth was Semele, who had offered him tea underneath the stage, and offered him welcome.

All of them had pointed ears and very large eyes—though Semele squinted with her large eyes through small spectacles. Their faces were freckled with greens and browns.

"Hello, Rownie," said Semele. "I am glad that you found us again, yes."

Rownie was not entirely glad that he had found them again. He felt nervous and unsettled. He sat up, and looked around, and was not reassured. Props and masks and musical instruments rattled in crates and made strange noises as they knocked against each other. Lantern light cast oddly shaped shadows, and the shadows rocked back and forth as the wagon moved. Everything around him was unsettling. It smelled like old clothes and paper.

"Hello," Rownie said, quietly and cautiously.

The tall, bald goblin said nothing. The one with the work-stained clothes also said nothing.

"They never say anything," said the goblin with spiky hair. Her voice was high, and her words jumped around like grasshoppers. "Patch never says very much, anyway. He's Patch. The tall one. She's Nonny. She really doesn't ever say anything. I'm Essa. We shared a stage last night, when I played Jack and you were trying to keep a giant mask from slipping off your head."

Rownie meant to protest that the giant mask had been in no danger at all of slipping off his head, and that he had worn it very well, thank you—but instead he said something else.

"You use coal." He did not mean to say that, but it bothered him enough to make his mouth say it without permission. He knew what made automatons move. He knew where coal came from. "The gearworked mule runs on coal."

"Fish-heart coal!" Essa protested. "We only use fish hearts to make Horace go. It takes several dozen to get a decent blaze going, but the fishmongers down by the docks sell them in bulk, and they work almost as well as the stuff made out of . . . larger hearts."

"Really?" Rownie asked. He didn't know fish hearts were flammable.

"Really," said Essa.

"Who's Horace?" Rownie asked.

"Horace is the mule," Essa told him.

"It is?" Patch asked. Nonny also looked confused. This was clearly news to them as well.

"Yes," Essa said. "I named it today. It needs a name, and I think it looks like a Horace."

Semele shushed everyone. "I am thinking that we should speak softly now. The Guard are marching alongside us, and the walls are not thick. Please sit down, yes."

Everyone sat down, except for Rownie, who was already sitting on the floor.

Patch stared at the wall in a dour and gloomy sort of way, as though he expected the Guard to arrest them regardless of what they said or did.

Nonny sat on a crate and patiently began to fold a piece of paper into different shapes. She made it crane-shaped, and then lizard-shaped, and then gear-shaped. Rownie recognized the writing on the paper. It was a copy of the notice advertising Tamlin Theatre, the one he had seen on the bridge.

Essa sat down, started fidgeting, stood up again, and climbed one of the cabinets nailed to the wagon wall. There she hung upside down by her knees and hummed a tune to herself.

Semele took off her spectacles, wiped them with a rag, and put them on again.

The wagon stopped. Essa stopped humming. Everyone listened.

Outside, Thomas shouted something brief.

"Is he calling for help?" Essa whispered. It was a very loud whisper. "I think maybe he just called for help." She reached into an open crate and carefully unsheathed a stage sword. "I couldn't really hear him, though. He might have said 'Bang, fallen dromedary.' It kind of sounded like that. What sort of signal do you think that is?"

"I do not think he spoke of dromedaries," said Semele. "I am thinking that he said 'The Changed call for sanctuary,' which signifies that we are at the litchfield gates."

Essa groaned. Patch sighed. Nonny folded the piece of paper into a mask shape.

"Do we really need to sleep in the litchfield?" Essa asked. "The best thing about coming home to Zombay is having a better place to stay than litchfields or crossroads or crossroads inside litchfields."

Semele shook her head. "The Guard marched us here," she said. "It is not safe to go home and show them where home is."

Rownie understood very little of the conversation, though he listened carefully. He sifted words through his head like fine dust through his hands, and he caught what he could. As the youngest he was used to piecing together his understanding from snatches of overheard conversations, and the rest he set carefully aside on the shelf in the back of his mind.

Metal shrieked against metal somewhere outside. Rownie didn't know what the noise was. He didn't think it was Graba's leg. He didn't think so. It sounded like a gate fighting against its own hinges.

The wagon started up again, and this time there was no sound of accompanying Guard-boots. It rode over an even rougher surface than the Southside streets, and everyone inside braced themselves against the walls and floor. They went over an especially violent bump, and Rownie bit the tip of his tongue when the impact knocked his teeth together. It hurt, but he didn't cry out. He tensed up his face with the effort of not crying out.

The wagon finally rolled to a stop. A small hatch in the front wall opened.

"We're here," Thomas said through the hatch.

"Where's here?" Essa asked, but he had already shut it again.

The whole wagon jittered while the gearworked mule folded back in on itself. Semele opened the door in the back wall and went outside. The others followed her. Rownie came last, but Essa stopped him in the doorway. She was still holding the sword.

"The Guard might be out there," she said in her loud whisper, "and they'll be unhappy with us if they see you, because Thomas said, 'Nope, officer, we don't have any idea where that mask-wearing boy might be, and he certainly isn't hiding underneath our very own wagon.' So keep hiding for just a second."

She peered outside and looked unhappy. She whispered curses under her breath. They were decent curses, spoken with a decent rhythm. "May the Guard Captain grow hideous ear hairs, and may his glass eyes both turn the wrong way around."

"Are they out there?" Rownie asked. "The Guard?"

"No," Essa told him, "but the graves are. We're in the litchfield." She left the wagon.

Rownie took a good-sized breath. He knew that Graba sometimes sent Grubs to run errands in the litchfield and collect the sorts of things that grow in grave-dirt. Blotches always came back with stories about fighting off ghouls. Rownie was sure that Blotches had made up the fights, but Blotches might not have made up the ghouls.

Rownie tried to feel like a giant. He adjusted his brother's coat on his shoulders and went outside.

Act II, Scene III

THE WAGON STOOD IN AN OPEN stretch of grass, surrounded by graves. The gravestones were all worn and
crooked, like teeth badly cared for. A single tree twisted its
branches through the air nearby. Rownie could see crypts,
mausoleums, and monuments packed close together near
the gate, at the other end of the field where important
people were buried. It looked like a small and separate city
unto itself.

The rain had stopped. The clouds had broken up, and
now they moved quickly. The sun was low in the sky. The
air smelled like fresh mud.

"We're spending the night here?" Rownie asked the
others. Old ropes dangled from the gnarled and unfriendly
looking tree. It was a hangman's tree.

"We are, yes," said Semele. "Tamlin cannot stay anywhere overnight within the proper city limits. Most of us,
along with other sorts of Changed, camp far outside the

city entirely—but we can also sleep in places that are not actually considered to be places. This is a place where living people come to visit dead people, so it will work very well as somewhere in-between and not exactly one thing or another thing."

"Oh," said Rownie. "What's a Tamlin?"

"It is a more polite word than 'goblin,'" said Semele.

"Oh," said Rownie. "I heard that the sun will burn you up if you stay too long in one place."

"Not so," said Semele, "though we would become sunburned."

The goblins began to bustle. They set up clotheslines and hung wet costumes up to dry. They built a fire and used it to boil a kettle of water. Rownie kept out of their way. He watched, and he wondered whether this was in any way a safe place to be. Not that he was accustomed to safety, but at least he knew the ways that Grubs and Graba were dangerous—or he used to believe that he knew. He thought about Grubs squinting at him with Graba's look and calling to him with Graba's voice. He remembered how little he actually knew about them, or their dangers.

After their bustling, the goblins all gathered together. Semele poured tea. Thomas brought out the bread basket.

"Let us see what sort of supper we can make from the materials at hand," he said. "We have dried things and pickled things—preserved for emergencies against our starvation—and we have bread that young Kaile offered us at the Broken Wall, which was very kind of her. However, the whole of our provisions will make an unbecoming meal for artists of our stature and accomplishment."

"Ate wild rat last winter," said Patch.

"That was unbecoming also," said Thomas.

"I kind of liked rat," said Essa.

Thomas made a harrumphing noise. He took the basket around to each member of the troupe. The gentleman's cane he carried stuck into the muddy ground a little as he walked, and he had to pull it free with every step.

"The bread also comes with a complimentary review of our performance," Thomas said. "The girl especially enjoyed *The Seven Dancers*."

"Oh good," Essa said, "though we really should change that name. There's only one of me."

"You imply the others well enough," Thomas said.

The basket came to Rownie, and Rownie cautiously reached in. He took a bread roll. His hand brushed against the bird mask that was still there.

He was, of course, hungry. The unpoisoned apple from the morning seemed like days and weeks ago. But he wondered what the dried and pickled things were. Maybe goblins ate moths and flowers. Maybe they ate children's toes.

Did you eat what they gave you? Graba had asked him. *Did you drink what they offered?* He wondered what would happen to him if he did.

They passed around pieces of salted riverfish instead of children's toes, and a few dried fruits instead of dried insects, and they sipped Semele's tea from wooden mugs while Thomas strummed a song on a battered bandore. The bread was still warm from the Broken Wall bakery, and it was tasty enough to make him want to crawl inside a bed-sized loaf and fall asleep. The riverfish was salty and chewy and excellent. The tea was lemony and sweet.

Rownie was impressed that the goblins shared food more freely than anyone in Graba's household ever did, and he resisted the urge to sneak some dried fruit into his only pocket. He could feel himself relax. His legs no longer prepared themselves to start running at any given moment. He stopped looking around for ghouls or the Guard. He let his toes warm up by the fire.

Then Thomas leaned toward Rownie. The old goblin did not pause in his playing, but he no longer seemed to be paying much attention to the song either.

"Tell me, young sir: Where in all the vastness of Zombay would your brother hide?"

Rownie coughed on a mouthful of tea, and spit most of it out again. Lemony droplets sizzled in the cook fire.

"Pardon the abrupt rudeness of my question," Thomas said, "but we have been looking for Rowan with some concern. We had taught him the language of masks, and he spoke it very well—better than anyone else in that amateur and unChanged troupe of his. Then we left Zombay for an important piece of business, far downstream. We returned to find his troupe arrested and undone, and Rowan himself escaped but missing. The Broken Wall is the very last place he was known to perform. Do you have any notion where he might be hiding now?"

The circle of goblins all stared at Rownie with their large, bright-flecked eyes. Rownie tried not to cough again. The world had just changed shape, and he didn't recognize the new shape it was in.

"You know my brother?" he asked.

"Yes, indeed," said Thomas. "A fine fellow, and a respectful student, though he also had a sense of mischief appropriate to our profession."

Rownie had as much trouble swallowing this as he had just had swallowing tea. He knew that his brother's life and world were larger than Graba's shack, but he didn't enjoy the thought that he knew so very little about it, or that these goblins might know Rowan better than he did.

"I don't think I should help anybody find him if he doesn't want to be found," Rownie said. "Thanks for the supper. Thanks for hiding me away from the Captain. But . . ." There was no polite way to ask this, so he did not ask politely. "Why should I trust you?"

Semele smiled. Nonny, of course, said nothing.

"Because we're nice?" Essa suggested.

Patch shrugged and looked dour. "Probably shouldn't," he said.

Thomas let out a sigh. It made his beard flare out in all directions. He stopped strumming the bandore and set it aside. "Because I swear to you, by the stage itself, by every tale and character I have ever breathed life into while treading the boards, by every single mask I have ever worn and offered the use of my voice, that we will not harm your brother, and that by finding him we can prevent harm from coming down upon a great many other people—ourselves included. I swear it by blood and by flood and by fire, and I swear it by the stage."

"Wow," said Essa.

Rownie was also impressed, but he still wasn't convinced. "Actors are liars," he said. "You pretend. It's kind of your job."

"No," said Semele. "We are always using masks and a lack of facts to find the truth and nudge it into becoming more true." She picked up a pebble from the ground, wiped it off with her sleeve, and held it out to Rownie. "Here.

This is more properly a way to say hello to the dead, who are stone silent themselves and therefore accustomed to a pebblish way of speaking. I do not think that Rowan is dead, but he is lost and therefore silent, and I know that this was his way of saying hello to your mother. So I will use it to say hello to you, yes—from him, and also from me."

Rownie took the offered pebble. It was greenish gray and egg-shaped. "Hello," he said.

"Welcome to our troupe," said Semele. "You may stay and perform with us. We will teach you the language of masks—though we must go about that carefully, yes, since maskcraft is more likely to bring about arrest and imprisonment than it once was. We must also go carefully because your former household will be hunting for you. You are still welcome. In exchange, please be helping us to find your brother before the floods come."

Rownie put the pebble into the only pocket of his coat. "He might be on the bridge," he said quietly. "I look for him there, and sometimes I see someone who looks like him, though it isn't ever really him. But maybe he's there."

"We have also searched the sanctuary of the Fiddle-way," Thomas said, "and we also have not found him. But we will keep searching. We are grateful for any help you can provide."

"What do you mean, his former household will be

hunting for him?" Essa asked. "We have to worry about old Chicken Legs? Again?"

"Yes," said Semele. "Please be cautious around pigeons. Tell me if you see them. Tell me if you dream of them, and shout if you wake up from such a dream."

"Pigeons aren't very clever," said Essa. "I mean, I knew an owl who could use doorknobs, and a pair of crows who played harpsichord together. They had terrible voices, but were really just fantastic at the harpsichord. But pigeons are so dumb and mangy-looking. Do we really have to worry about them?"

"Yes," said Semele. "Tell me if you dream of them."

"Speaking of dreams," said Thomas, "it is time we all went to our rest. We have a long walk before the show and the search tomorrow. Choose your masks for the morning walk, and then to bed. Here, Rownie. This one will be yours." He took off his hat, reached in, and removed a mask shaped like a fox's face. It had furry fox ears and a long fox nose, with whiskers.

Rownie took the mask and looked it over. It smiled with small, sharp teeth. Its fur was short, and coarse when his thumb rubbed it in the wrong direction. He smoothed the fur back again.

"You will also wear gloves and a hat," Thomas told him, "in order to hide your un-Tamlinish features. The Guard would be very unhappy with us for teaching maskcraft to an unChanged child. In this way you may hide with us, in full view and in daylight, and seem to be Tamlin yourself. Now, everyone to their rest. I'll see to the cleaning up. Rownie, find yourself a spare hammock in the wagon and keep the fox nearby while you sleep." The old goblin poured the rest of the kettle's contents over the fire. It hissed, sputtered, and steamed.

"Good night," said Semele.

The rest of the troupe mumbled their good nights. Rownie stood. He felt the fox teeth with his fingertips. He wondered if he would really be able to sleep in a litchfield, surrounded by graves and goblins and possibly ghouls, with a hangman's rope dangling in the tree branches and bird-dreams perched in the air, waiting to be dreamed. Then he yawned and followed Essa, Patch, and Nonny into the wagon. He carried the fox mask in one hand. With his other hand he checked to make sure the pebblish hello still sat safe in his pocket.

Act II, Scene IV

SEVERAL HAMMOCKS STRETCHED across the inside of the wagon, like sailors' bedding on a barge. Rownie found an empty one, set the mask underneath it, and figured out how to climb in. It took him three tries to manage. He had never slept in a hammock before.

He didn't think it would be possible to sleep. The bedding was unfamiliar. Straw and rope were both itchy, but in different ways, and he was accustomed to straw and not rope. But he had walked a long way when the day began and had eaten as good and filling a meal as he had ever tasted when the day was over. These two things together summoned sleep, and Rownie let it carry him off.

He dreamed that the city was also his face. The Fiddleway Bridge was the bridge of his nose, and it tickled as traffic walked across it from Northside to Southside, and from Southside to Northside. He woke up and flicked a bug away from his nose. He suspected that a Grub might have put it there, as a joke. Then he remembered that he was no longer in the company of Grubs. He opened his eyes.

Semele stood beside his hammock. She squinted at him. Dusty sunlight poured in through open window hatches in the wagon walls.

"Pigeons?" she asked.

Rownie blinked. He was only half sure where he was, and he wasn't sure at all what she meant.

"Did you dream of pigeons?" Semele asked.

Rownie shook his head. "No pigeons."

"Well, that is a good thing, yes."

Rownie tried to sit up. It wasn't easy, and he had to brace himself with both arms to manage. He didn't know how to get out of a hammock. Finally, he flipped the thing upside down and tumbled forth.

"Has the boy injured himself?" Thomas asked from elsewhere in the wagon. "Is he fragile? Is he dead? Have we lost our little fledgling actor already?"

Essa peered down at Rownie from among the ropes and rafters. "He's not dead," she reported. "Not unless he's the sort of dead who gets up and goes walking afterward."

"Good then," said Thomas.

Rownie got to his feet, embarrassed. Then he checked to make sure that he hadn't crushed the fox mask as he fell. The fox grinned, undamaged.

Semele showed him where breakfast was—a bit of bread and dried fruit, left over from supper the night before, and some runny egg yolk to mix with the bread.

The others were already awake. Most of them held masks in their hands. Patch had a half mask with a sinister-looking brow. Essa had two: one of a lady and another that looked heroic. Semele held a mask dyed bluish gray. It had high, sharp cheekbones and long, white hair. She sat on a crate and rubbed egg whites into the hair.

"That'll make the hair stick out in all directions," Essa explained. "She's playing the ghost, and she needs the ghost hair to flow as though moved by wind between worlds, so she shellacs it with egg whites first."

"I should have been doing this last night, yes," Semele said. She lifted the mask to regard her handiwork, and then added more transparent goop to the hair. "It will be droopy by the time we are finished with the walking."

Rownie wondered what "the walking" was, so he asked. "What walking?"

Thomas tapped the floor of the wagon with his cane, and he smiled a sly smile. "Rownie, we will now accomplish a very great mystery of our profession, something ancient and grand. We will mask ourselves and walk through the streets of Zombay, to the site of our performance. We will each walk alone, by several routes, and in this way we will find our audience. Those who take notice of you as you pass, those who follow to see where you will lead—without attempting to, say, *arrest* you—*they* are our audience. We will each of us lead them down to the docks and upstream to the very last pier of the Floating Market. Nonny will ride on ahead and meet us there with the stage itself. Do you know the way?"

Rownie nodded, because he did.

"Do you know *several* ways?" Thomas pressed him. "Will you lose yourself, once separated from the rest of us?"

"No," Rownie said. "I won't get lost. I don't get lost." He didn't always know where home was. Home used to be a shack that moved all over Southside, according to Graba's whim. But he always knew where he was in Zombay.

He wondered if Graba had already picked up the shack and moved it elsewhere. She probably had. It might be very far away, up in the hills of the southernmost part of the city. It might be very close. She might have leaned it up against the litchfield wall, near the gate, just outside. She might have moved it anywhere.

"Good," said Thomas. "Remember, Rownie—and all the rest of you—that what we do is important. This is a mystery of our craft. Carry yourselves with appropriate poise."

"This is what we always do whenever we forget to put

up posters," Essa whispered to Rownie. "Nobody would know about the show, otherwise."

Thomas pretended not to hear her, even though her whispering voice still carried. The old goblin took off his big black hat and pulled from it a mask with a high forehead and an iron crown. This was for himself. He also took out a smaller hat and a pair of gloves, and gave both to Rownie.

"Put these on," he said, "and the fox mask with them. You might also leave that tattered coat behind."

Rownie refused to take off his coat, but he put on the hat, the gloves, and the mask. The fox face smelled leathery, and it pressed oddly on the skin of his face. His nose itched. Then he stopped focusing on the mask, and looked through it. He saw his surroundings through fox eyes.

"Don't slouch," Thomas told him. "Not at all. Foxes are small, smaller than you are, but they do not slouch. Neither do actors. Stand and move with purpose. Move the way the mask would prefer you to move."

Rownie wasn't sure how the mask wanted to move, but he tried to stand up straight.

"Good," said Thomas.

The mask slipped down Rownie's face a bit. He tried to straighten it. Then he tried to ask whether he had it on properly, but Thomas shushed him.

"Don't speak while masked," the old goblin said. "Not if you can possibly help it."

Rownie took off the fox face. "Why not?" he asked. "I had lines to say when I was playing a giant."

"You did," said Thomas. "You delivered them with a certain amount of untrained talent—and *that* is why."

Rownie blinked. He didn't understand, and he wasn't willing to shelve his lack of understanding this time. "I shouldn't talk while masked . . . because I'm good at it?"

"Quite right," said Thomas. "As with a charm or a chant, the world might change to fit the shape of your words. Your own belief becomes contagious. Others catch it. You believed yourself a giant when you spoke as a giant, and so you became one. Your audience regarded you as one. They knew better, but they believed it anyway."

"I got taller?" Rownie asked.

"Everyone thought so," said Thomas, "so please don't declaim anything at all while wearing another face—most especially anything *about yourself*. Don't say any lines Semele did not write for you. And remember, always remember, that curses and charms have consequences. You set yourself apart from the world by changing the shape of it."

Essa put on both of her masks, one on top of the other. "The morning's wasting away," she said, trying to sound patient but not succeeding.

"Quite right," said Thomas. "Mask yourselves, everyone. And pay careful attention for any glimpse or news of young Rowan. Apart from the Fiddleway, the docks are the second best place in the city to hide."

Semele gave the egged hair of her own mask one final tug, and then put it on. Thomas and Patch did the same with their own. Rownie peered through fox eyes again. He tied the string above his ears and behind his head.

"Be on your several ways," said Semele.

"Break your face, everybody!" said Essa. She said it with so much hope and cheer that Rownie was sure he must have heard her wrong.

They left the wagon. The sun was up and bright. It had already burned away most of the morning fog.

Nonny waved from the driving bench, and then set off. The rest followed on foot, through the litchfield and through the gates. Rownie looked around for Graba's shack. He did not see it. Maybe she had taken it up into the hills. Maybe she was nowhere nearby.

The troupe separated, moving down different streets and alleys to the east and south. Semele took Rownie's gloved hand before he could choose his own way.

"Take care," she said behind the high cheekbones and waving hair of her ghost face. "If anyone puts a hand to you, run. It will mean that they know you are not Tamlin.

UnChanged folk do not touch Tamlin, as a rule. They seem to believe that it would give them freckles. You will be mistaken for Tamlin, and this should keep you safe, yes. But take care. While masked you will also be vulnerable to *changes*."

Rownie held the old Tamlin's hand, to show that he wasn't afraid of freckles—but he wasn't at all sure what she meant by vulnerability to change. "Is that bad?" he asked.

"It all depends," Semele said. She seemed to be smiling under the ghost face, but of course he couldn't tell.

She turned and went her own way. Rownie chose his.

*   *   *

All roads to the docks ran downhill. They wound and switchbacked across a steep ravine wall, with Southside above and the River below. Some of these streets were so steep and narrow that they had to be climbed rather than walked on. Stairs had been cut into the stone or built with driftwood logs lashed together over the precarious slope.

Rownie took these staircases on his own way down to the Floating Market. He remembered dockside errands he had run for Graba—mostly picking things up or bringing things down, and usually without ever knowing what the things were that he had carried. *Pick up a small package from a barge woman missing her left ear,* Graba might say. *Bring it back to me, now—but never be peeking inside it, and make sure it's her left ear that's missing.*

Rownie and Rowan used to run the dockside errands together. Rowan would usually have a spare coin or two, earned by singing on the Fiddleway or doing odd jobs for the stone movers near Broken Wall. He would use it to buy each of them some breakfast—a greasy fish pastry or a strange piece of fruit from foreign places—and then the brothers would eat their breakfast while sitting on some unused stretch of pier, dangling their legs over the side and watching the barges sail by.

Sometimes they made up stories about where the barges had come from, and where they might be going. Sometimes they imagined how fights against pirate fleets would unfold all around them, upstream and downstream, up and down the pylons of the Fiddleway Bridge, up and down the piers and the switchbacking streets behind them. Sometimes Rowan had enough to buy an extra fish pastry, and they would split the third one. He always gave his younger brother the larger piece.

Three pigeons watched fox-masked Rownie from a rooftop, and then turned away and pecked for seeds in the thatch. Rownie wondered if they were Graba's pigeons. He wondered if Graba had sent any Grubs on riverside errands today, to bring back fish heads or strange packages, or maybe to keep watch for him—or to keep watch for Rowan.

Rownie looked over his shoulder to see if Grubs were following. He saw others following him instead.

A small crowd of curious people had been pulled into his wake, diverted from wherever else they had intended to go and whatever they had intended to do. Some were old and some young. Some wore more expensive clothes and others less. They followed from a safe distance, watching him, wanting to see where he would go and what he might do.

It was *working*. Rownie carried an audience with him.

Not everyone noticed as he went by with poise and purpose in his mask. Some went about their business and were not at all distracted by a fox face. Their eyes missed him somehow. Their attention slipped around him. He was something strange, something that should not really be there, so passersby who were not his audience passed him by and assumed that he was not there if he was not supposed to be.

Rownie walked in daylight with a fox face over his own, and some people couldn't see him at all. He was hiding and proclaiming himself, both at once. He didn't know how this could possibly work, and he didn't want to think about it too much in case it *stopped* working, so he just kept moving. He let the fox mask show him how to move.

The audience was larger now. He could tell by the noise

they made, all packed together into the narrow, winding staircase. Rownie glanced behind him to see just how many there were.

He saw Grubs. He saw Stubble and Blotches and Greasy, all a part of the crowd that followed him. Stubble smirked.

The Grubs broke the charm. Before that moment, Rownie had been Rownie, and also a fox, and something that was neither one, and something that was both together. Now he was only one thing. The mask made it difficult to see, and he stumbled on a crooked stair. He tried to hurry without falling down the stairs entirely and rolling all the way to the docks, bloody and bruised.

The audience behind him thinned, no longer interested in whatever the masked performer might do next, or where he might be headed. The charm was broken. The Grubs had broken it with a look and a smirk, without even trying.

By the time Rownie reached the Floating Market, only Grubs followed him.

Act II, Scene V

A METAL LATTICE COVERED the whole of the docks. Each dome and arch of latticework held small openings for glass windows. The windows kept the rain out and let the sunlight through—unless the glass had fallen out, in which case it let through both sunlight and rain. The whole place smelled of fish, riverweed, and tar. Bustling noise and blunt, heavy smells rose up from the Floating Market and into the streets and alleyways of the ravine wall. Rownie could hear it, and smell it, before he finally turned one last switchbacking corner and saw it in front of him. Then he broke into a run. Grubs followed.

Narrow piers lashed to floating barrels jutted out from the shore and into the River. Small barges and rafts had been tied along each pier, packed close together, and each one was also a market stall. The Floating Market was a bigger, louder, and messier place than Market Square in Northside. Here mongers shouted, chanted, and sang about what they had to sell.

"Hammocks, comfortable hammocks woven from the finest braided squidskin!"

"Sugarcane and sea salt, good for charms and cooking!"

Rownie pushed into the crowds surrounding the downstream piers. He ran underneath the winch to the Baker's Cage, which was dunking some poor baker in the River for selling bread loaves that were too small or too large or too stale. Rownie forced his feet to learn how to move across the uneven surface that pitched and rolled with the River. He ducked and dodged between people. No one touched him or blocked his way, even when they failed to notice him otherwise. He hoped to lose the Grubs in the bustle and the noise before circling back and rejoining the goblins.

The fox mask felt heavy on his face, a brightly painted thing that shouted "Here I am! Here! Right here!"—but he couldn't remove it without showing off his own unChanged face beneath.

Fruit and fishmongers announced their wares to either side of him as he ran. The hard accents of upstream folk mixed and mingled with softer downstream syllables.

"Oceanfish! Riverfish! Dried and salted dustfish!"

"Rare pears and quinces! Figs and citrons from the shore!"

A meager fruit stall and a stack of barrels stood at the very end of the downstream pier, beneath an open stretch of iron lattice that had long ago lost its glass. The lone fruitmonger displayed baskets of sad-looking apples on a countertop, and didn't bother to announce them with a shout or a chant. He glanced at Rownie and then away again, uninterested.

Rownie turned around. The Grubs still followed him, unhurried. They had no reason to hurry. He had no other direction to run. He could face the Grubs or throw himself into the River—and the currents were very strong. No one ever crossed the whole River by swimming.

Stubble-Grub sneered as they drew closer. It was an ordinary sneer, just the sort of expression he would usually make. It was not Graba's look. Rownie didn't see Graba in his face, peering out through his eyes, wearing him like a mask.

Rownie *did* wear a mask. He stood like a fox, wily and proud. "You will not catch me," he said, and as he said it he knew that it was true.

He jumped onto a barrel, and from the barrel to the fishmonger's barge, where he kicked the rope and set the barge to drifting. Then he ran across the deck and jumped into the open air between the piers. His coat billowed behind him like a sail. He caught the railing of a barge across the way, and hoisted himself aboard.

The River took hold of the fruitmonger's barge, and it

drifted downstream. The monger cursed and paddled with a single oar, both furiously, but his curses were clumsy and unlikely to stick.

All three Grubs rushed to the open place where the barge used to be, and glared at the watery distance between them and Rownie.

Rownie took a bow. Then he slipped off the mask and stuffed it in his shirt. He walked calmly around to the front of the barge he had leaped to. The skipper here seemed to be fully preoccupied with selling fish-meat pastries that steamed and smelled delicious, and paid no notice when Rownie climbed down the barge moorings, just as though he had every right to be climbing down barge moorings. He rejoined the crowd and went looking for the goblin stage.

* * *

Rownie slipped between people. He moved quickly, but he did not run. He didn't want to look hurried. He didn't want to look like much of anything.

This was a fancier part of the Floating Market, a pier with the glass awning still intact above it. Those who gathered here sold more fragile things, like bolts of fabric and delicate gearwork—things that needed to be kept out of the weather. One barge displayed strange animals in gold cages. Soap makers invited passersby to smell their wares. A tall man with pale, deep-set eyes sold trinkets carved out of bone. Another barge-stall showed off small and cunning devices that did useless things beautifully.

Rownie glanced up at every face he passed, to see if anyone looked like his brother. He paid particular attention to people with beards, in case Rowan had painted or pasted on a fake beard to hide beneath. He looked at the barge crews on each deck, in case Rowan had signed up with a crew in order to escape Zombay and the Captain of the Guard. Rownie wondered if his brother would really set sail without him. He flinched away from the thought.

On the farthest edge of the upstream pier, just underneath the Fiddleway Bridge, a simple raft had been tethered. The goblin wagon floated there, lashed onto the raft.

Patch stood in front of the wagon, still wearing his half mask, with his arms folded in front of him. The goblin stared down a thin and scraggly looking man with a fish-hook charm around his neck. The man was shouting, and an audience had gathered around the argument. Rownie slipped into their midst.

"This is my pier!" the man shouted in a scraggly sounding voice. "I put on *my* show here!"

Patch raised one eyebrow, high enough to appear on his forehead above the mask he wore (which had its own eyebrows). "Show?"

"Yes, show!" the man said, pointing at Patch with

one finger as though trying to knock him over with it. "A *respectable* show, with no masks! I can swallow a fish for four pennies, and I'll swallow any other sort of scuttling creature for five. Can you do *that*, goblin? Bet you can't manage that."

The man had a bucket with him. Small things scuttled around inside the bucket. Patch reached in, took a handful, and showed the crowd a bite-sized crab, a snail, and a wriggling bait fish. He tossed the crab in the air, and then the snail, and then the bait fish. He juggled them all. Then he added two juggling knives, and their blades flashed in the sunlight. He caught the crab and the snail and the fish in his mouth and swallowed all three while catching a knife in each hand.

The crowd cheered. Rownie clapped. The scraggly man took a step forward, furious—but then he eyed the knives Patch casually held. He stepped back, snatched up his bucket, and stormed away.

Patch took a bow. The wagon wall behind him came smoothly down and became the platform of a stage. He somersaulted backward, landed on the platform, and started up a new juggling act while the other goblins started to arrive. Semele and Essa brought their own collected audience members to the crowd, and then slipped backstage through the wagon door.

Rownie wondered how best to follow when Thomas arrived and came to stand beside him. The old goblin carried himself in such a way as to be nearly unnoticeable, even while wearing a mask, even underneath his huge black hat.

"You've unmasked yourself," he said, his voice flat and unimpressed. "You have also neglected to bring an audience with you."

"I brought Grubs with me," Rownie whispered back. Thomas gave him a very blank look. "Children that Graba collects," Rownie clarified. "She probably sent them."

Thomas made a growling, grumbling noise in the back of his throat. "Excellent," he said, though he clearly did not think that this was excellent. "Please tell Semele once you make your way backstage, which you must do with a certain amount of stealth. Get behind those crates over there, put your mask back on—you haven't lost it, have you?—and then sneak underneath the stage. Knock three times on the wagon floor, and Nonny will let you in. You will assist her with backstage business for the rest of the show."

This was disappointing. "I don't get to be part of the play?" Rownie asked.

"You will certainly be part of the play," Thomas told him, adjusting his hat. "The part that goes on backstage. It is not as though you've had time or opportunity to learn lines, or even learn how to read. Your apprenticeship has only just begun."

"I can read," Rownie said, quietly.

"Don't worry," said Thomas, "I do understand that reading is hardly a common skill—"

"I can read," Rownie said again.

"—and not one we could possibly expect you to already know."

"I can read!" Rownie shouted.

A tall sailor with several braids poked Rownie's arm. "Shut it and watch the show," she said. "The goblin's juggling *fire.*"

"Ah," Thomas whispered, taken aback. "I see. Excellent. One less thing to have to teach you. Now please stop shouting and get under the wagon without being seen."

"Did you find out anything about Rowan?" Rownie asked.

"I have not," said Thomas, "though I have made many discreet inquiries known to observant people. Now please hurry backstage. The proper play is about to begin."

Rownie hurried. He hid behind crates, slipped his mask on, and then snuck underneath the stage. Hopefully, if anyone saw him sneaking, they would mistake him for a goblin. Maybe this was how goblins Changed. Maybe, if enough people already believed that a child was goblinish, then the goblinishness became real and true. Rownie reached under his mask see if his ears had become pointy. They had not. Only the fox ears were pointy.

He knocked three times on the wagon floor. A hatch opened. He climbed up and through.

Act II, Scene VI

BACKSTAGE WAS CHAOS DISTILLED into a very small space. Nonny did several things at once with ropes, levers, and various contraptions. Essa jumped up and down and hummed to herself for no particular reason that Rownie could see. Semele sat quietly in a corner with her eyes closed, but she still looked tensed and filled with potential force, like a coiled spring or a stone perched on top of a hill and preparing to start an avalanche.

Essa noticed Rownie. "You're here!" she said. "Good, because we're about to start. Patch just stopped juggling, and Thomas is out there giving the prologue for *The Iron Emperor*. I don't know why we call it that—the Emperor doesn't even show up until the last act, so it really isn't a good name for the play. We should call it something else. Try to think of something, okay? But meanwhile you should stay out of sight and pull whatever ropes Nonny tells you to pull. Not that she'll actually tell you anything. Pull whatever ropes Nonny points to. Okay, good. Break your face."

"Why do you keep saying that?" Rownie tried to ask her, but she had already slipped through the curtain and begun lamenting the woes of an ancient kingdom.

Rownie took off the hat and gloves, and set the fox mask aside. He approached Semele. He tried not to let the floorboards creak underneath him, but they creaked anyway.

"Some of Graba's grandchildren are here," he told her in a whisper. "On the docks. A few of them. Might not be in the audience yet, but they'll probably find it."

Semele's pale mask turned to look at him. "Thank you, Rownie," she said. "I will make the fourth wall stronger, then. This is certainly a tricky thing to be doing over water, but I will do it, yes."

She began to chant to herself. Then Nonny tapped Rownie's shoulder with her foot (her hands were both busy with a complicated crank and a set of bellows) and pointed her toes at a rope. Rownie pulled the rope.

The dragon puppet gnashed its teeth behind him.

Rownie dropped the rope, waved his hands in the air, and then stared down the dragon puppet to prove that he wasn't afraid of it. The painted dragon eyes looked back at him.

Nonny glared. *Wrong rope*, the glare said. She pointed more forcefully with the tip of her toe. Rownie pulled the next rope and felt the wagon shift under his feet. Flat, painted walls and towers unfolded to either side of the stage. The platform became a city.

"The moon is full," Essa said onstage, looking up. It was night onstage, even though the sun was shining above them. Essa said it, so it became true, and everyone believed it.

The Iron Emperor was a ghost story. Rownie caught glimpses of the play around the curtain edge, between pulling whatever ropes and levers Nonny directed him to pull.

Essa played both the Princess and the Rightful Heir. Patch played the Wrongful Heir—unless both the Princess and the Rightful Heir needed to be onstage at the same time, in which case Patch and Essa swapped masks.

Semele was the ghost of the old Queen, and she made her entrances in bursts of blue smoke and blue fire. This was always impressive, even backstage, even when Rownie could see Semele crouched out of sight beforehand.

Nonny set off the smoke and fire herself. She clearly didn't trust Rownie with any of the combustible effects. This was fine with Rownie. He worked the bellows on the music box instead. It played mournful, keening notes for Semele's ghostly entrances, after the bursts of blue fire and smoke.

Rownie heard gasps of fear and surprise, as though it really were midnight and not the middle of the day with sunlight bright and cheerful, as though Semele really were a spirit of the dead with hair moving in the wind between worlds and not just wearing a mask with egg whites making the hair stick out in all directions. Semele's high, commanding voice combined with music and smoke, and all of them together changed the shape of things.

Then everything went wrong.

First the music box broke. It broke loudly. It was supposed to give a long, mournful note, and instead it squawked like a peacock falling off a wall. This did not sound ghostly or mysterious. It did not sound like the wind between the worlds.

Nonny glared at Rownie. Rownie shrugged. He hadn't done anything wrong. At least he didn't think that he'd done anything wrong. Nonny pushed the unhappy music box aside, and the play went on.

They changed the scenery from city towers to the open sea. The sea was a blanket, gray and gauzy, and the two of them held opposite ends and flapped it up and down to make waves.

Then the waves caught fire.

One of the blue firecrackers went off, suddenly and all by itself. The sparks landed on the gauzy blanket, and the blanket burst into flames. Rownie and Nonny both dropped it.

Essa grabbed the sword of the Wrongful Heir away

from Patch, poked it through the burning blanket, and flung it away from the stage and out over the River.

Then the pigeons came.

Birds swooped down from all sides, snatched up the burning blanket, and kept it airborne. The fire spread and changed color from pale blue to an angry orange. It spread to the birds themselves. Pigeon feathers burned with greasy flame, and still they flapped their wings and flew above the audience with the burning sea-blanket between them.

The birds screamed and died and fell. The blanket broke into pieces, and fell. Fire came down on the audience. It came down on the nearby barge-stalls of the Floating Market. People screamed and pushed each other. Some fell splashing off the pier in their haste to get away from burning things. The awning of a barge-stall caught fire.

One pigeon smacked onto the stage and smoldered there. Essa flicked it away with the sword. The dead bird hissed and steamed where it struck the River.

Thomas took off his mask and looked sadly at their former audience. "The show is done, I think," he said to the rest of the troupe. "We had better hoist anchor before the crowd gets organized enough to have us lynched and drowned."

Semele came backstage. "Take us upstream, Nonny."

Patch and Essa untied the moorings that held the

wagon-raft to the pier. Nonny cobbled together some wire and springs, stuck four oars through it, and tied the whole contraption to the back of the raft. The oars spun around and pushed the wagon-raft upstream, away from the pier. They passed beneath the Fiddleway and over the spot where Rownie always dropped pebbles, where Rowan had taught him to drop pebbles for their mother. He felt for the pebble in his only coat pocket, the one Semele had given him in the litchfield, the one that was Rowan's hello. He thought about dropping it over the side to say hello to the mother he did not remember. Instead he kept the pebble in his pocket.

The screams and shouting of the Floating Market faded behind them. Rownie saw Stubble-Grub stand apart from the crowd. Vass stood with him.

"This was for me," he said. "The show was cursed, because of me."

Semele stood beside him. "This was for the both of us," she said in a voice that she probably meant to be comforting. "These curses were fashioned for you and me both."

Act II, Scene VII

THE WAGON-RAFT SPUTTERED UPSTREAM. Rownie sat on the edge of the roof, dangled his feet over the side, and watched the River go by. The city was out of sight already. The Fiddleway Bridge disappeared behind a bend. Rownie could not remember any place other than Zombay, and now he could no longer see it.

Nonny stood in the back and steered the raft by poking her paddle contraption with a pole.

Patch and Essa sat beside Rownie and dangled fishing lines in the water. They hadn't caught anything. Nonny's paddles scared all the fish away.

Semele sat up front, in the driving bench. Thomas sat with her, invisible beneath a big, black hat pulled low. Rownie didn't think the old goblin could see anything other than the inside of his hat, but then he pointed forward with his cane and shouted directions.

"There are rocks ahead! Nonny, kindly steer us to

starboard. Otherwise we are going to crash and sink and return the River's own face to the watery floor of its home. Then nothing could possibly prevent floodwaters from tearing down all of Zombay—which would suit my mood just fine, actually, so go ahead and steer for those rocks if it pleases you to do so."

Nonny steered around the rocks.

"What's he talking about?" Rownie whispered.

"The floods are coming," said Essa. "I mean, the floods are always coming, but they happen to be coming in a soon-and-immediate kind of way. Listen. I bet you can hear it."

Rownie listened to the River. He had heard it every day of his life, underneath and around all other noise. He knew its voice—and the timbre of its voice had changed. It spoke low and angry as the water flowed.

"There," said Essa. "You noticed."

"Maybe this is what it usually sounds like so far upstream," said Rownie.

"Nope," said Essa. "This is what it usually sounds like before a flood comes howling down the canyon. We should probably have warned more people on the docks. We didn't have very much time, I suppose, before our performance exploded, but I meant to tell a few skippers that they should maybe send their crew and cargo ashore, and up into the hills. Even a little bit of flooding will make things messy at the docks, and we're in for more than a little bit."

"I have already told such barge captains as will listen to Tamlin warnings," said Semele from the front bench. "They will spread the news. But we may yet be able to speak for the city, and thereby save Zombay from drowning."

"I am not presently inclined to bet on our success," said Thomas from under his hat. "There are more rocks ahead, Nonny. You may hit them if you'd like. Otherwise, steer to port."

Nonny steered to port.

Very little of this conversation made any sense to Rownie, but he didn't bother to ask clarifying questions. He felt surrounded by gloom and wished he had a big, black hat of his own to pull down over his face.

Graba had cursed the troupe and all of their doings. Grubs would follow wherever they went. Burning birds would fly screaming down at them until the stage and wagon caught fire, and they all burned with it—unless the River rose up in a flood before Graba had the chance to burn them. Bad things were coming—in water or in fire or both at once.

Semele pointed to a spot on the southern side of the ravine. "There," she said. "That is the place we should be aiming for, yes."

Nonny steered them to where Semele had pointed. She

tossed a grappling hook, grappled riverside tree roots with it, and roped the raft to shore. Then she stopped the spinning paddle contraption and climbed inside the wagon. The raft drifted at the end of its tether.

Rownie looked around. The place did not seem in any way special. "Why this spot?" he asked.

"This is our climbing place," Essa told him. "We need to get up to street level, to drive back into town."

Rownie looked up. The ravine was steep and very high. It did not look climbable. "We're going to climb that?"

"No, no, no, no," Essa said. "Definitely not. Nonny is going to climb and let down a rope, and then hoist the wagon back up to shore with a winch and crane. " She made it sound like a very easy thing to do. "The winch and crane are both already up there. Smugglers use them to carry things into Zombay without having to go through the dock wardens, but they haven't used it very much lately. I don't think so, at least. Hopefully there are no smugglers trying to use it right now."

Nonny came up through a hatch in the wagon roof. She had several tools in the loops of her belt. Without saying good-bye—or anything else—she stepped nimbly across the rope between the wagon and the shore, and started climbing.

"Shouldn't take too terribly long," Essa said. Her fishing

line tugged, and she started jumping up and down. "Hey, I got something! Fresh dinner, everybody! Fresh dinner!"

Essa hauled a mass of green tangles onto the raft. It landed with a splat.

"Hmm," she said. "Never mind. We could make a riverweed stew, I suppose, but the only time I've ever known a riverweed stew to taste good was when we left out the actual weeds, so I should probably just toss them back in."

No one else said anything.

Essa climbed quietly down to the edge of the raft and kicked her catch of weeds into the River. The green tangle sank out of sight. "I remember making wishes on riverfish, as a little girl," she said, "though I don't remember what the wishes were. And I was just as little as I am now, I guess. We don't get any taller, not even if we live for a thousand years."

"Do you usually live for a thousand years?" Rownie asked.

"No," said Essa. "Usually someone accuses us of child-thieving or butter-thieving or button-thieving or whatever a very long time before we get to be a thousand, and then they come for us with torches. Semele's the only one I've known who's anywhere near that old."

"Oh," Rownie said. He looked up. He couldn't tell if Nonny had reached the top of the ravine yet. Then two coils of rope came sailing down and smacked against the wagon, so he figured that she probably had.

Patch and Essa tied the ropes to the axle beside each wheel, and then untied the wagon from the raft. Essa gave a long, high whistle. The ropes began to pull. The wagon lifted, suspended in the air. Something shifted inside it and made a crashing noise.

"I'll try to salvage our belongings," said Thomas from inside his hat. "Essa, some help would be very much appreciated." He opened a hatch and let himself in. Essa followed.

"I will go in as well," said Semele. "Be careful, both of you."

Rownie and Patch watched the raft and River drop farther away beneath them.

"We're just going to leave the raft?" Rownie asked.

"Nonny'll build another one next time," Patch said. He gave up fishing and used his pole to push at the side of the cliff whenever the swinging, swaying wagon got too close to it.

Afternoon ended and became evening. The sun was going down. Colors of the dying day bounced up from the River, reflected. The River surface looked very far away now, but the top of the cliff seemed no closer.

Rownie looked at Patch sideways. He had something

he wanted to ask, but he thought that it might be a rude question, and he didn't know what words to use. Finally he just asked.

"How did you Change?"

Patch did not answer. He went on keeping the wagon clear of the cliff with his fishing pole.

Rownie waited. He waited for so long that he figured Patch would never answer.

"Used to have brothers," Patch finally said. "Lots. More than the family needed. Some left home to be soldiers. One left to study. Still too many. I was youngest, so Father took me to the wagons for Changing. Then he put me in the barn. Good luck to keep something Changed in the barn. A guardian. A thing to keep other monsters away. Stayed there a long time, keeping the sheep safe."

"How long?" Rownie asked.

"Don't remember," said Patch. "Years all blurred together. Left after a while. Joined a show. Not a good one. Did the Weasel Dance. Drop a dozen angry weasels in your pants and jump around while they fight. Crowds love it. Wore thick leather underneath to keep skin on my legs. Still uncomfortable. Weasels died in every show. All I got to eat, after. Semele's shows are better. So's the company. So's the food."

Rownie agreed. He was glad he didn't have to do the

Weasel Dance to keep himself fed—though a nightly meal of weasels would be better than no meal at all, and supper was rare in Graba's household. Meals with the troupe were very much better.

He heard Graba's voice in his head and memory. *Did you eat what they gave you? Did you drink what they offered?*

He checked his ears again to see if they had grown any pointier.

"How did the Change actually happen?" he asked, hoping for details. He wanted to know if he was Changing. He needed to know whether or not it would be a good thing if he did. "Was it from eating charmed food or something?"

Patch shook his head. "Can't remember. Too long ago. Sorry."

The sun set. The sky grew dusky and dim. The top of the ravine actually did seem closer now, and the view was just as wide and expansive as the one from the Fiddleway.

Something moved over Rownie's head, and he heard pigeons. He felt the tips of wing feathers brush against his face as a pigeon dove between him and Patch.

It circled back around and dove again. Patch smacked it aside with his fishing pole. It screamed at him, indignant. More birds joined it with answering cries, and the air became a furious, screaming mess of wings and sharp feet. *At least none of them are on fire*, Rownie thought as he ducked beneath another dive-bombing pigeon. He tried to get the hatch open, to take shelter inside.

In one sudden moment, three birds flew at Patch's face and knocked him off the wagon. He fell down and farther down.

Rownie crawled to the edge. He saw a splash far below them. That was all he saw.

Act II, Scene VIII

NONNY STOOD AT THE EDGE of the cliff and brandished a sling. She shot at the attacking birds until there were no more birds to shoot. Then the winch finished its work, and the crane hoisted the wagon up onto the ground.

Once they had untied the wagon, Nonny looped one foot through the dangling rope and hoisted herself back over the River, over the edge of the cliff.

"Find him," said Semele. "Take the raft we left behind. We will meet you at home, yes."

Nonny nodded, tugged on the rope, and plummeted down.

"He'll be okay, won't he?" Rownie asked.

"Patch can't swim," Essa said. She didn't say anything after that.

Rownie remembered the sight of Patch falling. Rownie watched him fall, and then watched again, and felt like he was falling with him.

In silence the troupe unfolded the gearworked mule and set off along Riverside Road, back toward the city. Rownie put his gloves and hat back on, to hide how unChanged he was.

They did not get very far.

At a crossroads, underneath the long shadow of a manor house and a few smaller shacks, a fallen tree blocked the road to Zombay. Children played a circle game near the tree, singing, "Tamlin, tinker man, beggar man, thief!" all together, all in one voice, and the one tagged "thief" had to chase the tagger around and around and around before the circle closed.

Rownie knew the game. He had played it before. He had run around the circle while Grubs sang the song. *Curse thrower, charm monger, Change maker, thief! False face, fox face, clock face, thief!*

The children stopped singing and stared at the wagon.

Rownie sat on the driving bench between Thomas and Essa. He peered out from underneath his own small hat and checked the faces of the children to make sure that none of them were Grubs. They weren't Grubs. They wouldn't be, this far outside the city.

"Can we go around?" Essa asked.

"No," said Thomas. "We cannot go around. The crossing road leads to nowhere important in either direction."

The old goblin climbed down from the bench and waved his cane angrily at the fallen tree.

"Why has no one in the village removed this roadblock? Why is no one doing so now? It is disrespectful to travelers to leave such a task until morning."

The oldest and tallest of the local children came forward. "This is a town," he said. "It's not a village." He said it with pride and disdain.

"Uh-oh," Essa whispered.

"What is your name, boy?" Thomas asked, planting his cane firmly on the ground and leaning forward.

"Jansin," the local boy said. He said it as though Thomas should recognize it, as though anyone and everyone should know who he was.

"This is not a *town*, young Jansin," Thomas said. "This is a crossroads with a fancy house nearby, and I flattered the place to call it a village. And you should not, incidentally, be singing and cavorting at a crossroads. You might disturb the graves of innumerable scoundrels, buried here so that they can never find their way home to take up haunting. It is unwise to show disrespect to the dead—or to travelers, who have very far to go. Please fetch someone to help remove this tree."

Jansin crossed his arms. He did not move otherwise. The other children gathered behind him.

"Why should we care about the crossroads-dead if they were all criminals?" he asked. "Why should we care about travelers if they're only goblins?"

"This is not good," Essa whispered. "Rownie, get ready to do something. I'm not sure what, but something. Probably grab Thomas and toss him in the back, so we can ride as fast as we can in some random direction."

Thomas drew himself up to his full height. The top of his hat almost reached the boy's shoulder. "Go on and wake the dead beneath you, if it pleases you to do so, but argue with me no further. My companions and I are weary and in grief."

Jansin marched up to the wagon and pounded on the side with one hand. "You've got masks painted here," he said. "So you're players, then. Goblin players. Put on a show for us."

The other smaller children cheered. "A show, a show!"

"We will not," Thomas said. "We are weary, and we have far to go tonight."

The boy tossed a coin to the ground. It was a large coin, and it looked to be silver.

Thomas stood over the silver, but he did not pick it up.

"Are you a merchant's boy?" he asked. "No. You could not be. No one from a merchant's household would throw wealth around so carelessly."

"My family owns the biggest coalmaker shops in the city," Jansin said. He said it with challenge, as though daring anyone to tell him that coalmaking was a dirty business.

"Ah," said Thomas. "A buyer and seller of hearts. One who believes that any heart can therefore be bought or sold. Well, coal-boy, we do play for coin, and almost any coin—but not for yours." He used the tip of his walking cane to flick the silver away. It rolled and wobbled back to Jansin. The boy scooped it up off the ground, flush-faced and angry. He threw it, hard, and knocked the hat from Thomas's head.

"Oh, this is bad," Essa said. "This is very bad." She tightened her grip on the reins. "I wonder if Horace could jump over that tree? He's never jumped before, but we could try it."

Rownie climbed down from the wagon on the opposite side, out of sight. He ditched his hat and gloves and circled around behind the crowd of children. Their attention was elsewhere. No one saw him in the dusk light. No one noticed Rownie standing behind them, just barely among them. No one noticed that he was unfamiliar.

Thomas, meanwhile, picked up his own huge hat, dusted it carefully, and set it back on his head. Then he unsheathed a thin sword from the length of his cane and held it such that the tip of the blade almost touched the tip of Jansin's nose.

"I will have an apology from you," Thomas said. His voice was calm, quiet, and cold.

Jansin glared, clearly afraid, clearly unwilling to take a step backward. The old goblin held his sword steady.

Everyone waited to see what would happen next.

Then a small hatch opened in the side of the wagon with a bang and a snap. Oil lamps burned in bright colors around it. Cheerful music played from one of the music boxes inside.

An intricate wooden puppet in gentleman's clothes popped through the open hatch.

"Welcome!" the puppet said in a voice that was almost Semele's. "Welcome, one and everyone! The evening's entertainment will now begin!"

The crowd of children pushed forward to gather near the puppet stage.

Thomas sheathed his sword and stood aside with a mutter and a grumble. "Unhitch the mule, Essa," he said. "Help me tie it to that tree. The metal beast had better be strong enough to move it aside."

Jansin smiled, smug. He had demanded a show from them, and now he had gotten his way.

Rownie looked for the silver coin. He couldn't help

but look for it. He had never even seen silver before. He didn't find it—one of the other smaller children must have picked it up first. Rownie gave up and pushed through the crowd to stand behind Jansin. The older boy might still be inclined to pick a fight, and if he fought the rest would fight with him.

The show began.

"I hope there's blood and guts in it!" one of the children said, hopping up and down on her toes with excitement.

An elegant lady puppet took the stage. Semele's voice sang a story behind it.

Rownie tried to watch the puppet show and Jansin at the same time. It wasn't easy, and he was distracted by other puppet shows in his head and memory. Rowan used to make shadow puppets against the walls of Graba's shack—when he still lived in Graba's shack. He could make shadows of sailing ships and animals, horses and goats and scampering molekeys. He could make silhouettes of people in tall hats or long gowns. Even the loudest and the rudest Grubs would watch and listen. Rownie always held the candle—a dangerous thing to hold over the straw-covered floor, but he was careful. His favorite shadow puppet was the bird, because that was the only one he could manage to make himself, with thumbs hooked together and fingers making feathers. Rowan had promised to teach Rownie how to twist his hands into other puppet shapes, but he hadn't gotten around to it yet.

The audience of children laughed at something on the little stage. Rownie shook his head, trying to shake out the shadows, and paid better attention.

Semele's voice sang a story about the lady puppet, who lived alone with a witchworked mirror. The mirror on the stage wasn't actually a mirror. It was just an empty picture frame with another puppet behind it. The Lady looked inside, and the matching puppet behind the frame mirrored her movements perfectly for as long as the Lady was watching—and then waved at the audience whenever the Lady looked away.

The mirror had been witchworked to show the Lady a young and childish reflection early in the day and an ancient reflection in the evening. The Lady learned how to reach into the mirror in the mornings and yank her own reflection through the frame and onto the floor. She did this several times, morning after morning, until many child puppets bustled around the stage with her.

Rownie wondered how Semele could possibly move them all at once. She was the only one in the wagon, so she had to be the only puppeteer, but each of the several puppets moved as though directed by a living hand. It was easy to believe that they were alive themselves, even though

Rownie could see that each was a thing made of cloth and wood, carved and painted.

In the story, the Lady kept all of these mirror children as slaves and servants.

> *"She had only herself*
> *For her own company—*
> *But she kept many selves of herself.*
>
> *It was they did the sweeping*
> *And all the housekeeping*
> *And dusted the books on their shelf.*
>
> *She harvested selves*
> *In the hours of each morning*
> *When reflections were not very old.*
>
> *She commanded them all,*
> *Her own selves while yet small,*
> *And herselves did just what they were told:*
> *Until the cruel Lady made coal."*

All the little puppets bustled offstage again. The Lady stood alone and put both wooden hands beneath her wooden chin. She looked harsh—mostly because of the way her sharp eyebrows were painted on. Then she shivered, her small arms wrapped around her puppet frame. The windows of her chamber grew dark and gray. Rain pattered against the back of the small stage. One of the young reflections came in with a broom, and the lady puppet loomed over her.

The next part of the show was unsettling to see. The Lady reached into the chest of her smaller self and removed something red. The little puppet fell over. There was no stage blood, or any other gruesome special effect, but Rownie still felt uncomfortable. He shifted his weight between one foot and the other. Some of the more squeamish local children squeaked.

The Lady put the heart into her fireplace, where it gave off a warm glow. She rubbed her hands together, enjoying the warmth. Then she placed a single metal gear inside the girl's chest. The little puppet stood up again—stiff and straight—and began sweeping the edge of the stage.

This was monstrous. Everyone knew what coal was and where it came from and what it was for. Everyone knew that automatons couldn't move without a lump of coal in their metal innards—or, in Horace's case, several tiny lumps of fish-heart coal. That was bad enough. To heat your house on a rainy day with coal, when any piece of wood would do just as well, was a monstrous thing.

Rownie noticed that Jansin didn't squeak or flinch or turn away. Instead he drew himself up to stand more stiffly, and clenched his fist a few times.

> *"Now, one slave girl witnessed*
> *The Lady take hearts,*
> *And that girl wisely feared for her own.*
>
> *She crept up to the mirror,*
> *The tall, witchworked mirror,*
> *And then was no longer alone."*

The little puppet reached through the picture frame and pulled out a twin.

> *"The day was still young,*
> *The reflections as well,*
> *And each one of them reached for another.*
>
> *Their hands passed through glass,*
> *And they clasped other hands*
> *Till the girls had a gang of each other."*

The puppets made more and more of themselves. Then the Lady returned with several slave-selves behind her.

They all fought. Puppets flew everywhere, tossed back and forth. When the fight was over, only three of them still stood—two rebel girls and the Lady. One of the girls pinned the Lady's arms behind her. The other girl reached into the lady's puppet chest and took out her large heart. They tossed the heart into the fireplace, where it burned briefly, and then went out. All the other little stage lights dimmed with it.

Rownie noticed, out of the corner of his eye, that Essa and Thomas were quietly returning the mule to its wagon hitch. The dead tree had been hauled aside. The road was clear.

Semele's song came to an end.

> *"Treat well your young selves*
> *Or they'll rise up inside you,*
> *And your heart will be overrun.*
>
> *So good night to you all,*
> *For the curtain must fall*
> *On this tale, which is over and done."*

There was silence. Then the little crowd began to cheer. "Blood and guts! Blood and guts!" said the smallest one, jumping up and down and clapping both hands together.

Jansin did not cheer or clap.

"My family takes hearts," he said. He did not shout, but his voice carried. It silenced the applause around him. "We take hearts from traitors and criminals and people who deserve it. We make them into coal. We should rip out your goblin hearts, but they probably wouldn't even burn."

Jansin took one step forward, and then Rownie kicked him hard in the back of the knee. *Nobody deserves to be made into coal*, he thought, but didn't bother saying so aloud.

The older boy went down. Rownie ran. He pushed other children out of his way and took Essa's hand as he reached the driving bench. She pulled him up. The puppet stage closed with a snap. Thomas cracked the reins, hard, and the mule launched itself into a gallop.

Their former audience shouted and threw stones, but the wild and angry noise soon faded behind them. After that Rownie heard nothing but the rattle of the wagon and the thud of Horace's hooves against the road, and he saw nothing behind them but trees.

Act II, Scene IX

SEMELE CLIMBED THROUGH a hatch in the front of the wagon. The whole troupe sat together on the driving bench.

"Slow down, yes," she said. "We are well away, and it is becoming dark and dangerous to ride so very fast. I will drive, I am thinking."

Thomas handed over the reins, but not without protest. "You can hardly see," he said. "You aren't even wearing your spectacles. How is it any less dangerous to let you drive?"

"This road is a very old road," Semele said, unconcerned. "I can drive along it well enough from memory." She slowed the mule down and steered it around a turning. "Please be letting me know if any new and unusual obstacles present themselves."

Thomas tugged his hat down over his face. "You should have let me give that insolent prig a warning cut. It would have been shallow."

Essa made noises of frustration and disgust. "Sure.

Perfect. Good idea. Shed a few drops of blood from a rich kid, at a crossroads, at night. Give that rumor legs and let it run around for a bit, and by the time we get back to the city, every single person will think that we ritually murder innocent children at crossroads in order to raise up an army of dead criminals with which to conquer all of Zombay. People already think we're child-thieves, so we really should try to avoid *attacking* any children. Even if they deserve it."

"We *are* child-thieves," said Thomas from underneath his hat.

"Only for very excellent reasons," said Semele. "And we are the children that we steal."

"Also, I don't really mind," said Rownie.

"While we are sharing recriminations," Thomas went on, "it was not, perhaps, the brightest notion to further antagonize that hotheaded coalmaker with a personal history about making coal and how very despicable the practice is."

"Hush yourself," said Semele. "The most useful thing for the both of you to be doing would be to make supper. It has been several hours since we ate. Rownie can stay here and keep watch for any more fallen trees in our way."

"I lost my hat," Rownie admitted. "I should probably get inside."

"Do not be worrying," Semele told him. "There is no one else on the road. Also, it is dark, and I think there will be a rising fog tonight. It would take very good eyes to see through all of this, and spot you for someone unChanged who keeps Tamlin company."

Essa and Thomas went below, grumbling. Rownie could hear further grumbling inside the wagon, though he couldn't hear what either one of them said.

He watched the road, a long and winding stretch of packed dirt surrounded by trees with twisting branches and roots. A fog did rise up, slowly covering the ground until the world itself seemed made out of fog, with only the wagon real and solid in it. Rownie couldn't see well enough to spot fallen trees, or any other roadblocks, so he just crossed his toes and hoped there were none. Semele still managed to keep the wheels on the road.

"That was quick thinking and quick doing," Semele told him. "I could see you in the audience, from spy-holes in the puppet stage."

"I just kicked him," Rownie said. "That's all."

"That is not all," Semele said. "You put yourself where you needed to be, and you had the foresight to do so. This was very well done."

Rownie savored the praise. He didn't get praise very often, so he was not entirely sure what to do with it. It made his face feel warmer in the foggy air. He didn't savor that warmth for very long, though. In his memory he saw Patch fall again, and again he felt as though he were also falling. He opened his eyes, and stared at the fog.

Something itched at the back of his mind.

"Graba has a lot of birds," he said. "All over the city, and even outside the city. We were a good ways upriver when her birds attacked us."

"Yes," said Semele. "Not all pigeons are hers, even in Zombay, but she does use very many of them."

"She's looking for Rowan too," said Rownie. "She was always asking about him, before."

"She would be, yes," said Semele.

"So why hasn't Graba found him? She keeps finding us. She keeps sending birds after us. She must be looking for Rowan, and her pigeons are pretty much everywhere, but Rowan's been gone for months. Why hasn't she found him?"

"I do not know," said Semele. She said it gently.

"Maybe he isn't here to be found," Rownie said. He didn't like saying that. He felt like he might make it true by saying it out loud. Maybe if he kept quiet, he could keep it from being true—but he couldn't keep quiet. "Maybe Rowan left the city already, without me. Or maybe he's dead."

"I am thinking that he is not dead," said Semele. "I wish that I knew where he was, and that I could tell you where. I do not know, but I am thinking he is alive."

"How can you tell?" Rownie asked, not yet allowing himself to be comforted.

Semele thought for a time before answering. "Your adoptive grandmother, she is very good at finding things. She is also very good at knowing when she should not bother looking. If she is still looking, then he is still somewhere to be found."

She steered them around another curve. Rownie stared at the fog ahead with less anxiety, beginning to trust Semele to know the road.

He thought about Rowan, hiding somewhere in the fog, somewhere even Graba's many pigeons couldn't spot.

Rowan used to disappear for days. Sometimes he would put a new troupe together, and try to rehearse, but this rarely went well. *They're too afraid of masks to put one on*, he complained once, while tossing several hellos over the side of the Fiddleway. *They're just willing to do a little play-reading, late at night, with the windows down and the shutters drawn, and someone playing a fiddle in the next room to cover the noise. What are they so afraid of?*

The Guard, Rownie said.

But what are the Guard so afraid of?

Rownie wasn't sure. *Pirates?* he suggested.

Rowan laughed. *No, I mean, why would a little pretending*

in front of a crowd . . . Never mind. I just wish the rest of my troupe had more courage.

I'm not scared, Rownie said. *Can I be in the next show?*

Not this one, Rowan told him. *There's no role good enough for you in this one. And I'll need you to be the one friendly face in the audience—if we ever get to stand in front of an audience.*

Rownie was disappointed, and Rowan noticed.

Let me hear the speech I gave you, the older brother said. *You've been practicing?*

I've been practicing, said Rownie.

He tried to remember that speech now, while he sat on the wagon bench with Semele. The first line came back to him—*I know my way, and I can guess at yours*—but he couldn't think of the next one.

Another thought itched at the back of his mind, on the shelf of things not yet understood.

"Thomas called the puppet show a personal history," he said. "Whose history?"

"Only mine," said Semele. "Our selves are rough and unrehearsed tales we tell the world. Hold on to something, yes, because there is an old tree root in the road ahead. There used to be, at least, and I am thinking it is probably still there."

The wagon wheels hit the root. Rownie's teeth clacked together. Thomas and Essa gave squawks of protest from inside.

"So what happened to the girls, later?" Rownie asked, trying to ignore the pain in his teeth. "The ones in the story? The ones who survived?"

"They never did agree on which one was first and which was a reflection of a reflection," Semele said. "One of them Changed and became Tamlin. The other learned witchwork, and she never, ever forgave the first for her Changing."

"Oh," said Rownie. "Oh." He had several thousand questions now. He asked the one he had asked Patch. "How did you Change? What happened?"

Semele hummed to herself. She seemed to be examining her own words before letting them loose.

"A Change is one big step sideways," she said, "in exchange for all of the small steps you might otherwise have taken. Yes. In most ways you *stop* changing, after a Change."

This was not much of a clarification. "But how does it happen?" Rownie persisted. "Is it happening to me?"

"No, Rownie," Semele told him. "We will not ever work a Change unwilling, on you or anyone. It is not happening to you, and will not happen unless you choose it. And we do need the assistance of someone both masked and unChanged."

Rownie didn't know if he was relieved or disappointed. He was not sure that he wanted his eyes to grow huge, his ears to grow long, and his skin to grow mottled with a thousand green freckles. But he did want to be something else, something other than he had been, and he thought that maybe monsters were safe from each other.

Essa opened the hatch behind them to offer up plates of vegetable pastries. The pastries smelled heavily spiced, and good. Suddenly supper became very much more important to Rownie than anything left on the shelf in the back of his mind. They all ate together, driving through the fog down Riverside Road.

ACT III

ACT III

Act III, Scene I

ZOMBAY EMERGED FROM THE FOG.

Rownie stared. He had never left the city before. It had always surrounded him. He had never seen it from the outside. He had never arrived in Zombay, until now.

Lights burned through the fog-filled dark. Constellations of lanterns and candles shone in uncountable windows. Street lamps—rare in Southside but common in Northside—cast warm light across cold paving stones.

The Clock Tower glowed above all. A glass moon ticked across a stained-glass sky on each face, illuminated from behind with lanterns, serving as a lighthouse to any barges sailing beneath the Fiddleway Bridge at night.

Semele drove them into Southside, into the medley of buildings built up over each other. Houses jutted out at strange angles, tethered with iron chains or buttressed with driftwood logs hammered into the brick and plaster to keep them from toppling over sideways. The misshapen mess loomed over them.

Rownie breathed more easily. He took in a lungful of Southside dust. It was comforting. It was home. Still, he kept careful watch for Graba's shack, knowing that it might be anywhere at all.

Gearwork hooves smacked the road at regular intervals. A few lonely street lamps lit either side of the lane.

"Are we near to Borrow Street?" Semele asked. "I am thinking that we are, but I would like to be sure."

"We're crossing it now," Rownie said.

Semele jerked the reins to the left, and Horace made a precise left turn. The wagon nearly tipped over. Rownie grabbed the bench to keep from flying off, and almost flew off anyway when the wagon settled back onto all four wheels with a crunching sound. Essa and Thomas made angry noises inside.

"Thank you," said Semele, unconcerned. "We have not far to go now, yes."

Rownie examined the familiar streets and avenues around them, trying to guess at their destination. "Where are we headed?" he asked.

"Home," said Semele. She drove through the entrance gate of the Fiddleway Bridge. "It is no small thing that we are showing you our home and inviting you to stay with us. It is not something that we very often do."

They drove as far as the middle of the bridge, and then Semele tugged the reins and pulled the wagon to a short, sharp stop.

"I cannot hear any other feet or wheels, in either direction," she said, "but please be taking a look around to see if there is someone nearby who might be watching us."

Rownie looked. He saw only fog and the empty causeway. The windows of the shops and houses on either side of the bridge were all shuttered and dark. It was very late. The Fiddleway slept.

"I don't see anyone else," he reported.

"That is a good thing," Semele said. She steered the mule and the wagon into a small alley on the upstream side. Then she made another turn, and pulled up in front of a featureless stone wall.

"Please open the stable doors, yes," she told Rownie.

Rownie stared at the wall in front of them. "I don't see any stable doors," he said.

"I invite you to see them," said Semele, and now he did. He couldn't see how he had missed them the first time.

Rownie climbed down, unlatched the tall pair of doors, and pulled them open. Semele drove the wagon through, and Rownie shut both doors behind them. The orange coal-glow of the mule's belly cast the only light inside. Rownie couldn't see much more than stone walls and old straw.

Essa stumbled out through the back of the wagon. "Home," she said. "Good. Somewhere there's a bed that isn't a hammock, and I'm going to find it."

"Not so fast, not so fast," Thomas called from inside. "We must return the masks to their places. The rest of the unloading can wait for tomorrow, but these should be properly cared for before anyone retreats to their own bed and blankets. Please show the boy where his own masks belong."

Essa stumbled back into the wagon, grumbling, and came out again with an armful of masks. The fox was among them, and also the giant that Rownie had briefly worn on the wagon stage.

"Here," Essa mumbled. "Take these two, and follow me."

Rownie took the giant and the fox, carrying one in each hand. Essa held the princess mask, and the hero mask, and a few others besides. She also had the half mask that Patch had worn that morning, which seemed a very long time ago to Rownie—years and centuries ago. Much had happened since.

He followed Essa through a passageway to an iron staircase. The staircase led both up and down. "We're going up!" Essa called behind her, from somewhere above.

"What's down?" Rownie asked. They were on the

Fiddleway, and Rownie didn't think that a bridge could actually have a downstairs.

"Barracks," said Essa, "all the way down the central pylon. People used to keep watch here for pirates and such, but now they don't bother. Some bits of the bridge still have skinny little windows for shooting things out of."

Rownie heard gearwork, turning and clanking against itself. He could almost hear Graba's legs in the noise. He could almost see her in the dim shadows. He almost felt her talon-toes opening and closing nearby. He was angry at Graba for her curses and birds, for Patch falling down and farther down, and he was afraid of Graba, and he was angry for being afraid and upset with himself for having made Graba upset with him. He pushed all of those feelings into a small and heavy lump of clay inside his chest, and then he tried to ignore the lump.

The staircase led up into a vast, towering space. Gears and springs, weights and pendulums all filled the center of it, turning slowly and interlocking. Crates and a jumbled mess of cloth and carpentry covered the floor. Rownie saw open wardrobes full of costumes, a workbench with all manner of tools, and several bookshelves. This was just as astonishing as anything else— Rownie had never before seen so many books together.

Lanterns burned high overhead, illuminating huge

circles of stained glass built into the four stone walls. Each circle showed a city skyline and a gray moon, half full. The sight was familiar, only now Rownie saw it from the inside out. He stared. His mouth was open. He didn't notice.

He stood inside the Clock Tower.

Act III, Scene II

"THIS WAY," ESSA CALLED over her shoulder. "Try not to get bonked by any moving bits of clock as you go." Rownie followed her, dazed.

It was then that he noticed the masks.

They covered both the upstream and the downstream walls. Rownie saw heroes and ladies, villains and charmers, nursemaids and gentry. He saw animal masks made of fur, feathers, and scaly lizard skins bristling with teeth. Most had been carved out of wood or shaped in plaster, but he also saw masks made of tin and polished copper, gleaming in the lantern light. He saw thin, translucent masks made of beetles' wings and carapaces, and wild masks made of bright feathers. He saw long-nosed tricksters and ghoulish false faces. Hundreds and hundreds of masks hung from nails by lengths of string, and every one of them seemed to be watching Rownie as he watched them.

Essa led him to an open space and an empty nail on the

wall. "Okay, the giant goes there," she said.

Rownie looked at the nail. It was high up, higher than he could reach. Essa handed him a long pole with a hook on the end. He carefully hooked the giant mask to the pole, lifted it up to the level of the nail, and got it to stay there.

"Good," Essa said. "The fox goes over there, near the books." Somehow she managed to point with one hand without dropping everything she carried. "You should be able to find it. The bunks are near the pantry. Feel free to snack before bed, if you're hungry, but don't eat too much of the dried fish or Thomas will have an extremely eloquent fit about how we are likely to starve if we ever need to hide out here for months and months—which does happen sometimes."

She went the opposite way, moving along the upstream wall and hanging up her own masks one by one. Rownie set off toward the bookshelves on the downstream side. He ducked underneath a ratcheting piece of tree-size machinery.

I'm inside the Clock Tower, he said to himself, still astonished. *The troupe lives inside the clock.* A place he had always known had turned itself inside out and become something mysterious and strange.

Something about this also bothered him and itched at

his memory. He couldn't think of what it might be.

The masks all stared at him with empty eyeholes or painted eyes. Rownie tried to stare back. He was good at staring contests. You had to have a good stare in a household of Grubs. But there were too many masks for him to meet all of their gazes, and he had to look where he was going to avoid being battered about by the tower's workings. This staring contest could not be won.

He found a place for the fox. It was low to the ground, so he didn't need a pole to put it back. He looped the mask's string over the nail and set it against the wall.

The fox mask moved. It lifted away from the wall and pulled against the string that held it there. Then it settled back into place.

Rownie took a step back. He stared. The fox stayed where it was and stared back at him. Rownie watched it awhile longer. He started to doubt that he had actually seen it move in the first place.

He looked around for the rest of the troupe and saw Semele and Thomas carry a mask between them. Rownie didn't recognize this one. It was carved out of stone, and had braided riverweed for hair. Swirling, painted lines of blue and brown covered the face. Rownie followed the two goblins to the center of the upstream wall, where they set the stone mask.

"This is the River," said Semele. "This is what we lost and left Zombay to find."

Rownie watched to see if it would move. It did not, but it looked as though it might move at any time. "A mask of the River?" he asked.

"No," said Semele. "It *is* the River, and *also* a mask. We needed to speak to the River, to give it a face and a name, so that we could ask it not to drown us with floodwaters. That was how it started, yes. This is the very first mask that I made."

Essa came to join them. They all watched the oldest mask while it did not move.

"Our craft and calling still has certain obligations," Thomas said. He spoke more quietly than he usually did. "It has from the very beginning, when those obligations were the whole of the craft. To ignore that part and purpose would be to lose the rest."

"What obligations?" Rownie asked without looking away from the mask that was also the River.

"To speak for the city," said Essa. "All of it. Northside, Southside, and the whole long length of the Fiddleway between them." She held up a wooden box and opened it. Inside was the city, carved from a solid block of wood and into the shape of a face. Half of the mask followed the winding sense of Southside and the other half obeyed the straight lines of the north. The bridge of the nose was the Clock Tower, where they all stood, and the small clock tocked and ticked in unison with the tower around them.

"Nonny made it," Essa said, "so Nonny really should be the one to open the box and say 'Ta-da!' or at least have a ta-da sort of look on her face, but she isn't here. Ta-da."

"We have always carved a new mask of the city, to speak for the city when the floods come," said Semele. "Zombay is a new place each time, you see."

"That's what you want Rowan to do?" Rownie asked. "Speak for the city?"

"Yes," said Semele. "This is why we taught him and why we are trying to find him. This is why everyone is trying to find him."

"Who wears the River, then?" Rownie asked.

"No one," said Thomas. "Absolutely no one. The River isn't a mask you can wear. Not any longer. It would wear you instead, if you tried. Much too old and much too strong. It would fill up an actor until they drowned in it."

"But it listens," said Semele. "Sometimes it will listen. And it might be that it will listen to you, Rownie, if you put on the mask of Zombay. Try it now."

"Me?" Rownie asked.

"You," Thomas answered. "We have been teaching your

older brother how to do this, but you do have a bit of talent yourself."

Rownie lifted the city mask and set it carefully over his own face. He pulled the string above his ears and behind his head. Through the eyeholes, he saw the others watching him, expectant. It made the back of his neck itch. He tried to swallow, but his throat was dry.

"Repeat after me," Thomas whispered. "Zombay River, oldest roadway, canyon carving, hear me."

Rownie looked up at the great River mask. Its eyeholes were dark, and he could see nothing through them. He wondered what would happen if he tossed a pebble through and how far it would fall and whether or not there would be a splash when it hit. He understood how someone could drown in that mask—and that the mask would not notice them as they drowned.

He repeated the line. "Zombay River, oldest roadway, canyon carving, hear me."

Nothing happened, and nothing continued to happen after that.

"Oh well," said Thomas. "Not to worry. Your brother should be able to manage, and we should be able to find him. Or else we might possibly track down another unChanged actor whom the Mayor has not yet arrested." He probably meant to sound comforting and optimistic, but he did not.

Rownie took off the city mask and set it back inside its wooden box.

"Why can't you do it?" he asked. He felt small and emptied out. He felt as though he should be better at this than he actually was. "Why does it have to be somebody unChanged?"

"We *have* done this," Thomas said. "Many times. But the city of Zombay currently excludes us, and we cannot speak for a place if we are not ourselves welcome there. This makes it very tempting to just sit back and let the floods do as they please, let me tell you. We, who have polished our craft to its very finest gleam, are now unable to perform the task that gave birth to that craft. But I am still fond of this unwelcoming place, and we still have our old obligations. So we teach our craft to someone who *is* welcome here and who knows their way around both sides of the city and the bridge in between."

Rownie *thought* he was that sort of person, but apparently he was not—or maybe he did not know enough. Thomas took off his hat, took out the Iron Emperor mask, and went down the length of the wall to find an empty space for it. He found one and put it there. Then the mask moved. A shudder of movement rippled through the other masks as well, and each one began to strain forward against strings, straps, and nails.

Act III, Scene III

THE IRON EMPEROR PULLED HARD enough to break its string. It fell. Then it stood up again. The air beneath the mask hardened into a body dressed in royal robes. It held a metal scepter in its hands.

"Well," Thomas said. "This is unsettling."

The mask revenant tilted its plaster face to one side, and regarded the goblin in silence.

"What would you, old vizard?" Thomas demanded to know. He rapped the tip of his cane against the stone floor with an impatient clacking noise.

The mask drew closer, gliding over the surface of the floor. It raised the scepter and struck.

Thomas moved quickly enough to keep his head, but not quickly enough to keep his hat. The scepter knocked it to the floor, and struck again. This time Thomas drew his cane-sword and parried.

"I made you myself!" the old goblin roared. "I have

played you many times to perfection! If you have any fighting skill, it is by my own instruction that you have it. And I will thank you not to heap further abuse upon my hat."

The Iron Emperor answered by knocking Thomas's cane-sword aside. The blade bounced away across the floor. The mask-figure shoved Thomas over backward with its free hand, and then it removed its own face. There was nothing behind the place where the mask used to be.

It reached down to mask Thomas with itself.

Rownie was already running and shouting. He reached Thomas's sword and snatched it up, but before he could put the weapon to any kind of use, the imperial mask shattered into several plaster pieces. Its body faded, the air softening until nothing stood there. The crown struck the floor, clattered and rolled, and then was still.

Nonny came up the staircase with a sling in her hand, and Patch came limping behind her. Rownie cheered to see the both of them, a wordless shout of happiness and relief. She had found Patch. Nonny had found him. Graba hadn't killed him with her birds.

"Thank you, my dear Nonny!" Thomas said as he climbed to his feet. "I am so very much obliged, and my heart sings to see you both safely here. *However*, I really do wish you had not smashed that mask. That plaster had soaked up well over a century of theatrical brilliance, and as I recall it was not an easy thing to make."

"Shut it, scowly trousers!" Essa came sprinting from the other end of the tower and knocked both Patch and Nonny to the ground with a tackling hug. Patch held his leg and winced. "I'm sorry, I'm sorry!" said Essa. "Are you hurt? Is it bad? Are you actually drowned and you just came back to haunt us? I hope not. I would hate it if you said even less than you usually do."

"Not dead," Patch grunted. "Just soggy. Found driftwood to hold on to."

A bird mask, now embodied, swooped above them and flew among the whirling cogs and levers of the clock. Another followed.

Thomas scowled. "Does anyone have the slightest idea why this might be happening?" he asked. "Anyone? And, Rownie, I will have my sword back, thank you kindly. You were very brave to reach for it, but please wait until we've trained you in the use of swordplay before you start swinging one of these about."

Rownie handed over the blade. "I get to learn swordplay?" he asked, his voice hushed and reverent. This was quite possibly the most magnificent thing that anyone had ever said to him.

"Yes, of course," said Thomas, impatient. "It is a skill

that actors must have. Epic combat unfolds in a great many of our performances."

"And this means that a great many of our masks know how to fight, yes," said Semele. "That is not currently a helpful thing."

More masks pulled forward, snapping their strings or yanking their nails from the walls. The air beneath them thickened into bodies, and embodied masks surged through the tower. Only the River remained in its place.

Another armed mask revenant approached the troupe. It seemed to be smiling at first, its carved expression light and jovial—but then the face tilted, and from that angle the same mask took on a look of sober intensity. It held a curved sword.

"This is Bidou," Thomas announced. "I will face him." The old goblin brandished his own blade with a flick of his wrist, and stood ready. His pride had clearly suffered in his earlier duel.

"Weapons," Essa said. "The rest of us need some. Rownie, there's a crate of sharp things right over there, and you should help me fetch them please."

She set off across the tower floor. Rownie followed. He tried to watch out for moving gears and flying masks and also other sorts of masks, but that was too much to watch out for so mostly he just ran.

Essa found the crate she wanted and pushed it over. Metal rang against stone as a great big mess of weaponry spilled out. "Grab a halberd," she said.

Rownie thought she had said "Graba" at first, and looked wildly around—but then he pieced together what she had actually said. "What's a halberd?"

"If an ax and a spear had babies, they would be halberds," Essa told him. "It's a pokey-pokey weapon for convincing things that are taller than you to stay back, please. Here's one." She handed it to Rownie and grabbed another.

A bird mask swooped down at her on silent, newly solid wings. Rownie shouted a warning. Then the mask broke apart in midflight. Essa ducked as pieces of it fell around her head.

"Nonny!" Thomas roared from across the tower. "Please do not break any more of our masks!"

"Especially not that one over there!" said Essa, pointing. "It's my favorite!"

"Which one?" Rownie asked. It was difficult to pick one mask out of the roiling chaos. "The blue one?"

"No, the one next to it, the one named Semmerling. Doesn't it look like a Semmerling to you? That blue one might also be my favorite, though. See its eyebrows? Those really are fantastic eyebrows. Oh, hey, be careful of the giant."

She shoved Rownie to the right and leaped to the left.

A giant boot came crashing down between them.

Rownie looked up. The mask he had worn looked down. It reached for him with new and giant hands. Rownie swung wildly with his halberd, tripped, stumbled, and rolled out of the way. Giant fingers grasped at the empty air above him.

Rownie picked himself up and slashed at the giant's boots, but the boots were thick and tough—or at least made of air pretending to be thick and tough—and the halberd only scuffed one.

"I bet you can't turn into a burnbug!" Rownie called up to the giant.

The giant ignored the taunt and reached for him again, to crush him or to eat him or else replace Rownie's face with its own and play at being a boy who had once played a giant. Rownie didn't bother running away. Its legs were very much longer than his, and it would catch him if he ran. Instead he took three steps backward.

The giant followed. A swinging, tree-size piece of clock swung into it and knocked the mask away from its imagined shoulders.

The giant body faded. The giant mask fell. Rownie caught it before it hit the ground. He looked up, grinning—but everyone else was busy, and no one had noticed his victory.

Rownie saw Patch throw juggling knives through ghostly

mask-bodies, convincing the masks that the bodies were not actually there, and then catching each mask as it fell.

He saw Nonny fire her sling in the air, trying to keep the bird masks away without breaking them.

He saw Essa face off against her favorites.

He heard Thomas roar invectives in the midst of his own duel.

He heard Semele keep several masks at bay with old and heavy words.

Rownie set the giant mask carefully down on the floor, hefted his halberd, and went to help Semele. He had to swing his way through many phantom mask-bodies to reach her.

Semele ended her chant, and dozens of masks clattered to the floor in a wide circle.

"This is an excellent curse we are fighting," she said. "This is a curse to be commended and admired. The bond between mask and performer has been twisted, and now they wish to play those who have played them."

"Why are so many of them after *you*?" Rownie asked. The words came out of him in a wheeze—his halberd was unwieldy, and his arms were starting to hurt. "Have you played them all?"

"No," said Semele. "I wrote them all, and many I have also carved."

Rownie swung at two long-nosed masks given bodies by this commendable curse—and then he remembered how the curse had been made and delivered. *It's a present of welcoming home*, Graba had said to Vass when she gave her the errand.

"I know whose curse this is," he said.

"So do I, yes," said Semele. A pigeon perched above them, on the workings of the clock. Semele spoke to it. "I see you there," she called. "I see you wearing the bird, as you wear the grubby children of your household."

The pigeon flapped its wings, and hooted.

Semele crossed her arms and sniffed. She did not seem concerned. "Child-thief? You do not care much for your charges while you have them—only when they are taken from you, when anything is taken from you. And you might have come yourself, yes. You send a sending instead, hiding inside birds and bullying us with our own masks. You might have come yourself to face me."

The pigeon gave an unpigeonlike shriek, and dove down at Semele.

"I do not have time for you," said Semele. "I did not come home to Zombay for you." She waved one hand, dismissing the bird. It flew away upward, shrieking, and vanished among the highest pieces of interlocking clockworks.

Rownie didn't have time to be impressed. The mask

revenants massed together into a silent crowd of bright colors and grotesque shapes, and they came for Semele. Some of the masks were hinged at the mouths and eyelids. These opened wide their eyes and gnashed their teeth. Semele sent most of them back with charms, and Rownie fought with the rest. He poked his halberd up at a ghoulish false face.

"I can break this curse," Rownie said, just as soon as he could pause and spare the breath. "I know where it is." He knew where Vass had put it.

"Then go," Semele told him. "I will hold them off, yes, while you go."

Rownie went.

Act III, Scene IV

IT WAS NOT EASY TO HURRY with a halberd. Rownie stumbled, and almost fell over. He realized that he might lose an arm or a leg or a head if he did fall. The ax at the end of the pole was very sharp. He dropped the thing with a clatter and a crash, leaving it behind, even though many embodied masks stood between him and the staircase. There were too many to fight. He dodged instead. He tried not to be dazzled or distracted by the sudden movements of dancing and fighting and bold colors and swirling shapes in all corners of his vision. He made for the stairs, reached them, and went down.

It was dark in the stables, with Horace all folded up and hiding the coal-glow. Rownie felt his way along the wall, found the door, and undid the latch. He went out into the fog. He went through the alley and up the stone steps to the front doors of the Clock Tower. The doors were sealed and shut. The chains had long ago rusted together, and could not be unlocked.

Tied among these thick and thickly rusting chains, Rownie found a leather bag. Smoke poured out of it, of a darker shade than the fog. He didn't want to touch it. He wished that he had kept the halberd, so he could poke at the thing from a distance or at least carry it away on the end of a long pole. But he didn't have a halberd. He only had his hands.

Rownie took a deep breath, took the curse bag with both hands, and ripped it away from the Clock Tower doors.

He expected the thing to be hot and burning. It wasn't. The curse bag was cold, and the *cold* burned him.

He turned around and looked for the nearest space between buildings where he could toss the bag down and into the River—flowing water was the very best way to wash off a curse—and then he stopped.

The fox mask stood before him, directly before him. It wore a fine suit, with leather gloves and leather boots. The fox nodded, polite, a gentleman's greeting.

It did not attack him. It did not peel away its own fox face to mask Rownie with. It did not come any closer. Instead the fox stood aside, and gestured with one gloved paw.

Rownie went cautiously in that direction. He crossed the street, holding the curse bag as though it were an egg or a fallen, fledgling bird. The coldness of it hurt. It seeped into the bones of his fingers and made his hands feel as though they were no longer his.

The fox followed him.

Together they went down an alleyway on the downstream side, farther away from the Clock Tower. Rownie reached over the edge of the low stone wall and dropped the curse bag. It fell into the fog, and into the River, and was gone. Rownie hoped that the River didn't mind. He rubbed his hands together to chase away the cold, and they started to feel like they belonged to him again.

"Thanks," he said to the fox—but the fox was not there. The empty mask lay faceup on the stones beside him. Rownie picked it up. He wore it around his neck by the string, without putting it on.

* * *

Back inside the Clock Tower, many masks lay scattered on the floor. Rownie glanced at the upstream clock face, and saw that the moon was setting. Night was ending. The morning would be here soon.

He found the rest of the troupe where they had taken refuge among the bookshelves.

"Well done, Rownie," Semele said.

"Yes, very well done," said Thomas, poking cautiously at a fallen mask with his cane-sword. "I am curious to know what it is you actually did, of course, but I can wait."

Essa set her halberd aside and picked up the mask with the excellent eyebrows. "That was very strange," she said. "I got a little bit in character whenever one of my masks came close to me, and that made it really hard to fight when they were the weepy sorts of characters who made me feel like swooning."

"Whereas I remain filled to the very brim of my hat with tragic intensity," said Thomas. "Excuse me, please." The old goblin left for some other part of the tower.

"Best we not disturb him for a good long while," said Semele. "We should put these masks back where they belong, and perhaps chain them in place . . . but the task can wait for morning, yes. It will require care. Some of them should only be handled with the left hand, and we will first have to gather many lengths of short, stout chain. We should wait, to be sure of doing it properly. To bed now, yes."

The troupe stumbled toward several small bunks near the pantry shelves. Rownie went with them. He found a bed of his own. He took off his coat, because the bed already had blankets. Both his folded coat and the fox mask he stashed underneath the bunk.

Rownie was tired beyond tired, but he did not sleep. Not yet. His thoughts spun like the workings at the center of the Clock Tower—always moving, always turning, never still.

He wondered what Graba might know about Rowan and his whereabouts, what sort of hints and inklings she might have. He wondered how he could possibly get her to tell him what she knew. Graba did not share, but she did *bargain*, and Rownie had gone on many market errands for her. He knew how to bargain. To offer a deal he needed to have something Graba wanted—and he had one thing that she did.

He made a choice, and after that he slept.

Act III, Scene V

MORNING LIGHT CREPT THROUGH the downstream clock face. A stained-glass sun ticked upward from the very edge of a glass horizon.

Rownie woke after just a few hours' sleep. The rest of the troupe still seemed to be unconscious. He heard snores and saw lumps of blankets on the other bunks. He couldn't tell who was snoring. It might have been Essa.

He sat up on the edge of his bed. The masks still lay on the floor where they had fallen. Rownie put on his coat, picked up the fox mask, and found himself a breakfast of dried fruit and cold flatbread in the pantry. It felt strange to take the food. It felt like stealing, even though he knew that it wasn't, even though Essa had told him that it was perfectly fine to snack from the pantry cupboards. In Graba's household, every hungry mouth was on its own.

He sat on the floor, chewing shriveled fruit pieces with

the fox face on his knee, and he wondered where Graba might have moved her household. He needed to find her—or to find someone else who could find her.

He had a message for Graba.

Rownie stood and tucked the fox mask inside his coat. This also felt like stealing. He told himself that it was only borrowing, and hoped he would have the chance to bring it back. Besides, the fox had followed him last night, all on its own.

He took in a long breath, and headed for the staircase.

"Good morning to you, Rownie," said Semele, before he had gotten very far.

Rownie jumped. "Morning," he said, nervous and guilty feeling.

Semele did not look as though she had slept. She picked up a fallen mask and considered it sadly.

"Cracked all the way through," she said. "It is not a hopeful sign to see this one broken. We carved it from a block of alder, offered willingly by a living tree. Cypress is best for mask making, but alder is also good, and a very fine wood for boats and bridges. The Fiddleway has wooden bones of alder wood, in among the stone."

Rownie reached for the broken mask. Semele handed it to him. The face looked simple at first, unadorned and without expression—but then he saw a smile when he held it at one angle and a thoughtful frown when held another way. The eyes also changed, seeming to close at a downward tilt.

"What's it a mask of?" he asked.

"This is the UnChanged Child," Semele told him, "though it is changed now by breaking. By tradition this is the very first face a new maskmaker attempts, and the very last face to be mastered."

"But you didn't start with this one," Rownie said, remembering.

"No," said Semele. "I began with the River, and worked in stone. I am a fair bit older than most traditions are."

Rownie gave her back the UnChanged Child. "I'm sorry it's broken," he said.

"This is no fault of yours," she told him. "I mean that truly, yes."

"Thanks," Rownie said, "but all of this might still be mine to fix. I think I can help find my brother, or at least get a little news about him."

Semele nodded. "Take good care of the fox. It is old, that one."

"I will," Rownie promised, and felt sheepish about concealing the fox in his coat. "Wish me luck."

"Break your face," Semele said, with sincerity and kindness. "That means luck," she added. "I do not actually remember why it means this, but it does." She gave another mournful look at the broken face in her hands.

"Oh," said Rownie. "Good, then."

* * *

Outside it rained in sudden spurts and starts. The sun peered out from behind clouds, as though shy. Then it hid itself again, and again the sky rained. All the ordinary traffic of the Fiddleway kept their heads down. Beasts and persons, both gearworked and not, seemed to see only their own feet in front of them. They paid no notice to the boy who emerged from an alleyway and climbed the stone steps of the Clock Tower.

A single pigeon stood perched on the rusting chains. Rownie had hoped to find one there. It pecked at the chains with a little tap-tap noise. It looked confused. It looked as though it wondered where the curse bag had gone.

"I took it," Rownie told the bird. "I broke it. Tell Graba, if you have a little piece of Graba in your head. Tell her I broke the curse, and you can tell her something else besides."

The bird stretched both wings and scratched underneath one of them with its beak. It acted like it didn't notice Rownie and could not be bothered to notice him.

"It doesn't have any of Graba," said Vass, behind him. "It has a piece of me instead."

Rownie turned around. He stood like a giant and stayed

where he was. It helped that he stood a few steps above Vass, on the stair. This brought them eye to eye.

"You broke her curse?" she asked, marveling at him. "She is going to make a birdcage out of your skin and bones, and keep only the ugliest birds inside you, and she won't ever clean out the cage, either."

Rownie ignored her smugness. "I have a message for Graba," he said. "You can deliver it—in person, or with birds, or with whatever else you use to send messages."

Vass almost laughed at him. "Tell me your message, sir," she said, bemused and still smug.

Rownie stood like a giant. He stood like Rowan. He was not embarrassed. Vass could laugh just as long as she liked, and it would not matter to him. Not very much.

"Tell her to meet me at the Southside Rail Station." The station might be in Southside, but it felt like Northside. It followed different rules. In the station she might be out of her element—less terrifying, less strong.

Vass saw that Rownie was serious, and she looked less bemused. "When?" she asked.

"Now," Rownie said. "I'm on my way now. I'll meet her there." He still didn't know where Graba had moved her household, but he did not need to know. Graba could come to him instead.

Vass watched Rownie carefully. Something shifted behind

her eyes. She nodded and spoke with something a very little bit like respect. "I'll pass your message on," she said.

"Thank you," said Rownie. He turned away and went down the steps.

Vass called after him. "She hates to lose anything that she thinks is hers. You know that. She won't let you get away from her again."

"She can try," Rownie said, and he almost laughed. He remembered what it had felt like to cast a mask-charm at the Floating Market. *You will not catch me*, he had told the Grubs, and he had made it true. He still had the fox with him. He could still avoid being caught.

* * *

Rownie crossed the bridge. He passed dueling fiddlers as he stepped into Southside and smelled Southside dust. He walked between the fiddlers, through the music of their duel. Neither one seemed to be winning.

He passed members of the Guard as they marched. It was strange to see so many of them in Southside. Here they moved slowly, with many stops and adjustments of direction. It was common knowledge that the Guard hated Southside—all of Southside—with its curved, winding streets and unusual angles. They much preferred the precision of Northside avenues, over which they could always move quickly.

Unlike the Guard, Rownie understood these winding streets. The soles of his feet spoke their language. He could move quickly in Southside.

He passed pigeons, many pigeons. The birds watched him sideways, and he nodded to each of them.

"The rail station," he said. "Tell her I'll meet her there."

The birds made hooting noises, and flapped their wings. Rownie thought that they heard him and understood him— but he couldn't be sure of it, so he told the same thing to every new pigeon that he saw. *The rail station. Tell her. Tell Graba.*

Rownie came to the old station gate, and slipped through the bars. He went in as though he knew where he was going, as though he had every right to haunt that place, as though he were something to be afraid of. He almost believed that these things were true.

✳ ✳ ✳

The Southside Rail Station was empty, save for pigeons, and for Rownie. Dusty, cloudy sunlight came through the glass panes of the ceiling. It slid down over the brass finish of abandoned railcars, and fell on the curved rust of wrought-iron benches. Pigeons swooped down from the dangling clocks and passed through the dusty light, circling, silent.

"Graba!" Rownie called out into the wide and dusty air.

"I have words for you! Come hear them yourself!"

Tell me about my brother, he said silently. *Come and tell me anything at all about Rowan, in exchange for the chance to catch me. Come help me find him.*

At first only silence answered. The light faded, and raindrops pattered against the glass overhead. Then gearwork noise echoed throughout the station, bouncing back and forth between stone floors and columns. He thought the sound might be Graba's legs making their long strides through a station corridor, but it wasn't.

A single railcar drove through the tunnel at the far side of the station and came to a halt on the track only a few paces from where Rownie stood. It was an actual, working, gleaming railcar. Thick curtains covered long glass windows on the inside. The mirrored brass finish had been polished and scrubbed, so there was hardly any tarnish on it anywhere.

Rownie stared at the splendid thing. He took a few steps closer. *How did it get here?* he wondered. *They must have pumped the water out of the whole tunnel.*

The railcar doors opened. The Captain of the Guard stepped down to the platform. Vass followed behind him. She wore no expression on her face at all.

"Rownie of Southside," the Captain said. "The Lord Mayor of all Zombay would speak with you."

Act III, Scene VI

ROWNIE WAS UNPREPARED for this turn of events. He stared at the Captain of the Guard with his mouth hanging open.

The Captain marched forward. His boots rang out against the polished stone floor. His irises tocked and ticked in small, perfect circles as he focused on Rownie and bore down on him. The Captain took hold of Rownie's arms and steered him toward the railcar before Rownie could even think about slipping on the fox mask and declaring himself uncatchable.

"You are not under arrest," the Captain said. "You are suspected of having broken lawful edicts of this city, but you are not under arrest. The Lord Mayor would speak with you."

"He's telling the truth," said Vass.

Rownie glared at her. "I gave you a message for *Graba*."

Vass nodded. "And it would be so much worse for you

if she were here instead," she told him. Her voice was cold. Her face was cold. Both were glass-smooth and offered nothing to hold on to.

She went back inside the railcar. The Captain of the Guard pushed Rownie through the doorway after her, and shut the door behind them all.

Gold lanterns burned inside. Red cloth covered the floor, the windows, and the far wall in hanging curtains. A long dining table took up most of the space, and a sumptuous meal of roast goose and fresh fruit took up most of the table. Rownie could smell the crispy goose skin. He had never in his life eaten goose, but at that moment he very much wanted to try it.

Chefs had refletched the bird and posed it upright. Its wings stretched out to their full span across the table. Both the wings and neck had been filled with tiny filaments of gearwork. The wings flapped slowly back and forth. The beak opened and sang a little tune. It was pretty. It did not sound much like a goose.

The Lord Mayor of Zombay cut chest meat from this seemingly live bird, and took a bite.

Rownie stared. The Mayor smiled at him from behind his trim beard and his chins. He only looked a little bit like his statue. He was not a very wide man, but he did have a few extra chins.

Vass sat down beside the Lord Mayor as though she had every right to be there, or anywhere else that she might choose.

"Welcome, young sir," said the Mayor. He wore many rings. They knocked together when he moved his hands—and his hands were always moving. "I would like to offer you employment in my own private troupe of actors."

As he spoke, the railcar shuddered and moved. Rownie felt it slide over rails and down into the tunnel, down under the River, down in a long, straight line toward Northside. The cooked goose flapped its wings and sang another song.

✳ ✳ ✳

Rownie thought about the Mayor's words. He tried to make them make any kind of sense. "Your own *what?*"

"My own private troupe," the Mayor said again. "I have a few of them here with me." He clapped his hands. The red curtains at the front of the railcar opened to reveal a small stage. Three performers stood, bowed, and began to tell a story in dumb show. They were all three masked. One mask had been painted with sharp, straight lines, like a tattooed map of Northside, and crowned with a coronet of small towers—Zombay towers, not as they currently stood, but as they used to stand. The mask wore a stern and kingly expression. The other two masks looked like fish.

Rownie forgot about how tasty the goose must be, and

he almost forgot how absurd it was that Vass sat beside the Lord Mayor of Zombay. "You outlawed acting!" he shouted. He tried to keep his voice down. He couldn't. "How can you have a troupe of your own, and a stage of your own, when you just outlawed them all?"

The secret play continued to unfold. The three performers didn't seem to notice or mind that their audience was talking among themselves rather than paying proper attention. They went on telling their silent story, indifferent to whomever might be watching.

"It is true," said the Mayor. His rings knocked together. "I did outlaw the theater. But just because a thing is not good for *everyone* doesn't mean that I should not still enjoy it, if I can." He winked. "Have an almond."

He tossed Rownie a small, spiced nut. Rownie caught it. Outrage boiled up inside him, but he tried to swallow it down. Shouting at the Lord Mayor was probably not a clever thing to do, especially under the cold and ticking watchfulness of the Guard Captain, so Rownie ate the almond instead. He chewed it furiously until there was nothing left.

The Mayor continued with his meal and offered nothing more to Rownie. Vass ate a few grapes and also offered nothing. The railcar moved smoothly on its track, somewhere underneath the River.

"Floods are coming, you know," the Mayor said. He said it to Vass and not to Rownie.

"I know they are, sir," said Vass.

"They are expected to fill the ravine entirely and rise up as high as Southside—which is, of course, lower and closer to the River. The damage will be very severe." The Mayor shook his head, and his chins, at the tragedy. "I am doing what I can to prepare. I am pulling together enough funds to rebuild, after the flooding has come and gone. We will return the city to its days of glory, and we will help South-side recover—and help to make it a more orderly place."

"That is very good of you, sir," said Vass. She ate another grape. Rownie found it impossible to tell whether she was pandering to the Mayor or honestly agreeing with him or possibly making fun of him. Her voice and her face were still glass-smooth.

"Thank you," said the Mayor. "I do what I can. But meanwhile, before the devastation comes, it would be sensible to be in Northside. We should remain high out of reach of the coming floods—most especially since I have masked performers to address the River on behalf of the north." He waved one hand at the stage and at the actors, without actually looking in their direction. "You understand this, of course," he said to Vass. "It is why you came to me."

"Yes, sir," said Vass. "It is." She looked at Rownie. There

was something new in her face. "Graba hates rivals," she said. "She hates them. I'll have to leave Southside anyway, someday, just as soon as I learn enough witchwork from her. There used to be lots of witchworkers in Southside, but now there's only her. She makes certain that there's only ever her." The glass-seeming surface of her voice cracked. She spoke as though she wanted Rownie to understand. "I need somewhere else to go. I'll go north. The Mayor already promised me a house of my own. A grand house. I won't have to sleep on straw. I won't have to climb through windows. I won't have to run errands for Graba, not ever again. All I had to do for it was tell the Mayor about you."

"So you see," said the Mayor, turning to address Rownie directly, "it would be best to avoid the southern half of the city until after the floods have come and gone, and obviously the bridge cannot grant sanctuary in this case. In the meantime I offer you employment and a place in my household. It is a great honor to serve as a member of the Lord Mayor's Troupe. They have their own stage in my house, you know, and it is far more grand than that little goblin platform you walked on recently. Do you understand what an honor this is?"

Rownie started laughing. He couldn't help it. He tried not to, and that set off a rapid cascade of hiccups.

The Mayor's smile slipped a little. He took a few more

bites of goose. Vass stared at Rownie as though he had turned into some sort of fish. The three actors continued their pantomime without noticing anything else.

"I do understand," Rownie said, between hiccups. "You want it to happen. You *want* Southside to drown, so you can make it like Northside, and just another part of Northside. You arrested everybody who ever wore a mask—even me—to make sure Southside will drown."

The Mayor struck Rownie with one ring-covered hand. It hurt.

"I speak for this city, child," he said. His voice was cold. "I do. No one is going to wear a piece of plaster and pretend to speak for Zombay. No one is going to negotiate on behalf of Zombay—not to armies or to diplomats or to the River itself—unless I appoint them to do so. That is my office. I will uphold it, and you will show proper respect. Do not pretend to be other than you are."

"What am I, then?" Rownie asked. It was an honest question.

The Mayor did not answer, and Vass did not answer, because something smacked against the side of the railcar. The Mayor moved a red curtain away from one long window. Lantern light from inside the car illuminated the curved brick of the tunnel outside.

Birds flew through the tunnel, surrounding them, overtaking them. Pigeon wings knocked against the window's glass.

The Mayor looked annoyed. Vass looked terrified. Her eyes were wide circles. "It's her," she said. "She's coming for us. She won't let us get across."

"It's only birds," said the Mayor. But pigeons flew by in dozens and droves now. The railcar shuddered as they threw themselves between the wheels and the track.

Rownie should have been scared. He wasn't. He stopped thinking about the birds, because the crowned mask of Northside had slipped from the lead actor's face. That face was as familiar to Rownie as any could be.

The railcar shook and slid to a halt. The lights inside sputtered and went out.

"Rowan?" Rownie asked in the dark.

Act III, Scene VII

THE MAYOR SHOUTED SOMETHING. Rownie heard him, but he did not listen, and he did not notice what the Mayor said.

Vass chanted. A single lantern bloomed on the wall. She took it down. The Mayor gave orders to the Guard Captain, who drew his sword and used it to shatter a window. Rownie ignored them all. He stared at Rowan. Rowan stared at nothing. The loose strap of the mask was down around his neck. The mask itself sat empty over his chest. The play had been interrupted, and now none of the three players moved.

The Mayor put a chair under the broken window and ordered the Captain through. The Captain climbed through. He pulled Rownie behind him.

Rownie fought. He yelled. He put everything he had, and everything he had ever had, into pulling in the opposite direction. He shouted his brother's name, which was his own name made tall, and Rowan went on staring at nothing in a calm and empty sort of way. Rownie went on fighting, but it did not matter. The sleeve of his dust-colored coat ripped as the Guard Captain pulled him through the empty space where the window used to be, out into the tunnel. The ground underfoot was thick with dead birds.

The Captain of the Guard called back to the Mayor and told him that the tunnel was empty, and that the wheels of the railcar were so caked with bird pieces that they could not be made to turn again. The only way back into Northside would be to walk there.

The Mayor climbed out the broken window. Vass went with him. She carried the single lantern she had spoken to.

By that lantern light, Rownie saw Graba.

* * *

Graba perched on her talons, on the railcar's roof. She climbed down with one long step, followed by another. She loomed over them with her legs extended, until it seemed that the space of the tunnel was made out of Graba and only existed to suit her purposes.

The Captain of the Guard raised his sword. Graba spoke to him in a low chant. "Your workings are broken. Your sight, it is broken. Your vision is filled with the sight of its breaking." She said this as though it were already true, and it became true as she said it. Springs sprung and gears shattered in the glass workings of his eyes. He cried out, stumbling, and dropped the sword.

He also dropped his grip on Rownie's arm. Rownie crept slowly back toward the wreckage of the railcar.

"There, there," said Graba, as though comforting the Captain. She reached with one talon and knocked him against the tunnel wall. He slid down, his hands covering his broken eyes.

Graba turned to Vass and the Mayor. She looked at Vass as though deciding whether or not she might be edible. "Hello, granddaughter," she said. "Hello, little rival."

Vass stood very straight. "Hello, Graba," she said. Her voice sounded cracked and fragile, but it also sounded brave. "I'm not your grandchild. None of us ever were."

"But you *are*," said Graba. She reached for Vass with one hand to tuck a lock of hair away from her face and behind one ear. The hair fell forward again. "What else could you be? I took you in, all of you, when you had no one else. I made you a home when your elders had drowned or starved or run off without you, abandoning all of you. Who else might you belong to, now, if not your Graba?"

Vass held up her chin. "Thank you for that. But I'm still not your grandchild."

Graba gave her a long, considering look, and crossed both arms in front of her. "I'm thinking that you may be right in this," she said, her voice full of wonder and hurt. "You may not be mine any longer. Go on to Northside, then. Make the Mayor keep his promises, and make him suffer if he doesn't give you that house of your own. You've made this choice, so make it a sticky one. No good will come of it if you go wavering—not from him, and not at all from me."

The Mayor chose that moment to speak up in an affronted and important-sounding voice. "Do not refer to me as though I were not here, witchworker."

Graba smiled. She looked delighted. She looked as though she had just crunched her teeth down on the tastiest egg imaginable.

"The Mayor is *not* here," Graba told Vass. "I would hurt him if he were here—and then he would never make good on his bright promises to you. This is my gift, and it will be my last one. To enjoy it, you should be running. The whole of this tunnel will fill up with floodwater, and very soon. The floods are coming. They are coming today."

Graba leaned forward and squinted hard with her squinty eye. "You should tell his mayorship that even if the River wipes Southside as clean as an uncarved gravestone, I will still make sure and certain he never, ever rebuilds it to his liking. Southside is mine. Tell him I said so, now. I would tell him myself, but *he is not here*. I would hurt him very much if he were here. I would set beautiful curses on him."

The Mayor sputtered in his outrage. Vass put the lit lantern in his hand. "Please start running, sir," she said. "You aren't here. You shouldn't be here." He sputtered further. Then he turned and ran away northward, into the dark of the tunnel.

Vass paused. She looked at Rownie. Rownie wasn't sure what she meant by that look. Then Vass helped the Guard Captain to his feet, and the two of them followed the Mayor. All three vanished down the tunnel's throat.

Rownie remained in the dark, with Graba. He tried to remember how to breathe.

Act III, Scene VIII

GRABA SPOKE IN A VERY LOW CHANT. The brick and stone of the tunnel's wall began to glow green, like the color of young burnbugs. In that green glow she looked down at Rownie as though examining a piece of market fruit for fungus and rot. She smelled familiar, a musty and feathery smell.

"You have a message for me, runt?" she asked. The air between them stretched as tight and tense as fiddle strings.

Rownie felt fear, bone-deep and burning. He did not run. He knew that there could be no running from Graba, with no hiding places in the tunnel and her long legs striding easily behind him. He showed Graba that he would not run, and he gave his message.

"I wanted your help to find Rowan," he said, "but then I found him. He's in the railcar. He didn't move, and he didn't know me when I shouted. He just stood there, all empty-looking, and I don't know what's wrong. Please help him. I'll come back with you. I'll be your grandchild again."

He tried to stand like a giant.

Graba stood like Graba, and grunted. "You still smell like thieving and tin."

"I haven't Changed," Rownie told her. "I'm not a goblin. I'm not a Changeling. I'll come back."

Graba reached up with one talon, took hold of the railcar, and ripped away the front of it. Metal shrieked against metal as she tore it apart. Rownie flinched. It was a painful thing to hear.

The three actors did not react to the sight or the sound of Graba's coming. She nudged the two in fish masks aside with her foot, and then squinted at the third.

The Northside mask still dangled from Rowan's neck. Graba plucked it from him, dropped it on the tunnel floor, and stepped on it. Rowan did not seem to notice. He stood very still, and looked away at nothing much.

"What's wrong with him?" Rownie asked.

Graba tore open the front of Rowan's shirt. A red scar, sharp and clean, ran down his chest. Rownie knew what that meant. He tried very hard not to know what that meant. The world changed shape around him, and this new shape was not what it was supposed to be. Graba scowled and spat.

"Puppet," she said. "His mayorship thought he could

talk to floods with puppets. He's more a fool than he deserves to be, now."

"Can you help?" Rownie asked. "Can you give him back what they took?"

"No," said Graba. "And I won't be taking you back, either. You might be mine again, but I no longer need you. No time now to teach you enough to be useful, and Graba knows better than playing with puppets. The River won't dance on a puppeteer's strings, so none of the floodings can now be avoided."

She climbed up and over what was left of the railcar.

"Help him!" Rownie shouted after her. She had to be able to help him. She could reshape the world with her words. She was herself a force of nature. She was Graba.

"Run away, runt," she called back. "Run back to Semele. Run away from the River. I'll be carrying my home to higher ground, now, and herding most of Southside with me." The squeak of her leg receded as she made her way back up the tunnel.

* * *

The curved brick walls still glowed from Graba's chant. By their light Rownie picked his way through the wrecked railcar. He came to stand beside his brother, who did not notice him there.

"Rowan?"

Silence.

"It's me."

More silence filled the space around them. Rownie breathed cold silence into his lungs. He stood and stared at his brother, just stared, there in the tunnel underneath the River, under the place where they had always thrown pebbles. He searched Rowan's face for any flickering sign of recognition or welcome. He couldn't tell what he saw there. He didn't know whether any slight movement of the eyes or mouth meant anything at all.

Rownie felt like he was the one who had been hollowed out.

Water dripped down from between the bricks in the curved ceiling. It dripped faster. A droplet struck the side of Rownie's face. He forced himself to move. He took his brother's hand and led him out of the railcar wreckage. Rowan followed easily, without resisting, without any will of his own.

Rownie went back for the other two, the ones in fish masks. He pushed them northward. "Go," he said. "Start running. Don't stop until you're out of the tunnel, and after that find some stairs to climb." They listened to him. He hoped they could both outrun the flood.

Rownie and Rowan went south. They edged around the side of the railcar, stepping over broken birds and broken glass. Air moved through the tunnel's throat in a low moan. Rownie couldn't tell what sorts of things it said.

They moved around the circumference of pits and holes where the dirt had caved in beside the tracks. The air around them smelled like wet, dead dogs and rotting fish. Rownie heard splashing from the largest pit. He didn't look over the edge, but he did call down to whatever splashed there.

"The floods are coming," he said to the pit and the ghouls and the diggers. "Take care. Floods are coming." Maybe they heard him. Maybe every haunting thing dug itself to safety, out of the River's reach—if any place could be out of the River's reach.

Drips from the ceiling came more frequently now. Water seeped between bricks. Rivulets ran through the dirt under the track and grew wider. The dirt disappeared. The rails disappeared. There was only water, up to their ankles and then to their knees. The burnbug light from Graba's chant began to fade.

Rownie and his brother trudged through the rising water. They moved slowly. Rownie didn't think they could make it all the way back to Southside before the tunnel flooded entirely. He didn't know what to do. He felt useless and helpless and small. He felt like he needed to be something other than himself, so he took out the fox mask and put it on.

In the fading, failing light, Rownie saw the tunnel around them through fox eyes.

He saw a door in the tunnel wall. He remembered what Essa had told him about the Clock Tower stairs: that the staircase went all the way through the central pylon, down and farther down.

"I know my way," he said to Rowan, "and I can guess at yours." He still couldn't remember the rest of that speech, but he knew as much as he needed to. He pushed through the tunnel, moving as a fox might move, and pulling his brother behind him.

They reached the door. It was locked. This didn't matter much, because the lock was also rusted through and broken. Wood and metal complained when Rownie pushed, but the door still opened. In the dark behind it Rownie found an iron staircase. He found the handrail and shook it hard. Nothing broke or came loose. It didn't seem to be too badly rusted.

Rownie and Rowan climbed the iron staircase, up and farther up.

They passed rooms that used to be barracks, now empty. Small amounts of cloudy sunlight crept in through narrow windows. The light seemed bright and blinding after the gloom of the tunnel.

Rownie was angry now. The momentum of anger

pushed him forward. His skin was angry and his bones were angry and his heart was angry at the vertical scar on Rowan's chest, where Rowan's heart used to be.

They climbed up through the center of the Fiddle-way, up into the Clock Tower. Rownie led his brother out among the masks and the tree-size gears and pendulums, out beneath the clock faces of stained glass.

He pulled the fox mask from his face and shouted for help.

Act III, Scene IX

SEMELE CAME OUT FROM behind the bookshelves. Essa jumped down from somewhere overhead. Patch limped from the pantry, with Nonny helping him. Thomas approached with his cane's tip clacking against the tower floor.

"You found your brother!" the old goblin said. He whipped his cane through the air. It made a celebratory swishing sound. "Magnificent! However did you manage it? Never mind, never mind, tell us the tale over some refreshment. Welcome back to us, young Rowan. Your timing is absolutely flawless."

Rownie said nothing. Rowan said nothing. Semele was the first to notice the two different sorts of nothing that they said.

"Hush," she said to Thomas. "Hush."

She lifted a torn corner of Rowan's shirt, and then set it back in place to cover the scar.

"He doesn't know who I am," Rownie told her. He felt his anger drain away. He didn't want it to go. He fought to keep it. Anger kept him moving. It kept him warm. But now words fell out of his mouth like cold pebbles. "He just stands there with his ribs all empty and he doesn't know me."

Semele took his hand and shook her head. "He does remember you," she said. "To be heartless is to be without his will, but not without himself. He is still there. He still knows all that he knew." Her voice grew softer and more careful. "But intention and volition have been taken. He has no momentum beyond what others give him."

"Can we find his heart?" Rownie asked. "Can we put it back?"

Semele did not say no. She did not need to. She did not say anything else.

Rownie shook his head. This was not true. He would not let it be true.

"He looks very calm," said Essa, clearly trying to help and not knowing how. "Heartlessness doesn't look too unpleasant."

"He's a puppet," said Thomas, disgusted and sad. "May the Mayor eat rancid liver paste, and suffer crippling pains. The floods are coming, and the city has no one to speak for it."

"The floods are coming right now, actually," said Essa.

"I would have said so earlier, and I was on my way down here to say so, but then it seemed rude to interrupt because Rownie's brother got his heart taken away, and I am so very sorry about that. But now I need to tell you that the floods are here already. You can see the water rising from the upstream clock face."

"You can also hear it," said Semele. "Listen."

A sound like endless and ongoing thunder filled the space around them. It grew louder. It came from the waters beneath the bridge, and it came from the oldest mask. Floating hair of braided riverweed moved in a mane around that mask.

Thomas whacked the floor twice with his cane. "Places, everyone!" he roared. "Essa, back up the winding stair with you. Ring the tower bells, if those old things are still capable of ringing. Anyone who hears that sound, and remembers what the sound is for, will head for the hills. Nonny, help me throw a few sandbags behind the tower doors. Locks and chains won't keep the River out if it rises this far. Patch, come and help us if your injury will allow it—or else keep us company if it will not. Rownie . . ." Thomas paused, and then shook his head. "Rownie, look after your brother."

"What if the whole bridge comes crashing down?" Essa asked.

"This bridge has stood for a very long time," said Thomas.

"Because people keep rebuilding it!" Essa countered. "Not because it never falls down! It does fall down sometimes!"

Thomas hit the floor again with the tip of his cane, as if to demonstrate that it was solid. "Places, everyone!" he roared again. Then he whispered to Semele. "A chant or a charm to help hold these stones together might not be amiss."

"I suppose that would be useful, yes," said Semele.

"You inspire great confidence," said Thomas. "I'll compose my last words while we stack sandbags."

Everyone moved, except for Rownie and his heartless brother. Rowan seemed perfectly content to stand in place, whether or not the bridge came crashing down beneath them.

"Are you listening?" Rownie asked him. "Can you hear what we're saying? Do you know what's going on?" He poked Rowan's arm and got no reaction. He kicked his brother in the shin, and got no reaction from that either— and then he really wished that he hadn't kicked him. He felt his own heart slam against his rib cage, as though it wanted to get as far away from this place as it possibly could.

The stones and metal workings of the Clock Tower groaned. Rownie thought he also heard music in the sound, but he couldn't be sure. Then the flood noise grew louder. It roared and echoed in the unseen throat of the River mask.

The roar shifted something inside Rownie's chest. An idea came to him.

"Come on," he said. "You might not have any will or momentum, but I think I can find you some." He took his brother's hand and led him to the very first mask, the mask that was also the River, the mask no performer ever wore. The open mouth of the mask thundered. Rownie was very much afraid of sinking down and drowning in its bottomless eyes.

He took it from the wall. It was made of stone and very heavy. He stumbled under the weight of it.

"Rownie?" Thomas called from the other side of the tower. "Whatever you are doing, I doubt very much that it is a good idea!"

"Probably not," Rownie answered, but he did not return the mask to its place. He looked up at his brother. "I'm going to put this on you. I really hope you don't mind. But if anyone can keep from drowning under this, it's you." He climbed onto a crate and slipped the mask over Rowan's face.

* * *

The River mask merged with Rowan's skin. The inked and painted lines of it flowed across his face. He threw back his head, opened his mouth, and gave one wordless shout with an immense and canyon-carving voice. The sound was a bridge of water between the mountains and the sea.

Rownie jumped down from the crate and shouted against the swirling, rushing onslaught of noise. "Rowan!"

Rowan looked at him. His hair moved around his head like riverweed swept by strong currents. His eyes had become vast and full.

"Hi," Rownie said to his brother, who was also the River. "Please don't flood."

"This is not a very good idea!" Thomas called as he hurried across the tower floor. "Where is the city mask? Nonny, fetch the city mask! Hurry up, hurry up, hurry up. The source of all our craft seems to be underway, and no one has rehearsed for it!"

Goblins gathered. Nonny offered the mask of Zombay. Rownie took it, but he did not put it on, and he did not look away from the bottomless eyes of his brother.

"Do you remember your first line?" Thomas prompted him.

Rownie nodded. "Oldest road. Older brother. Hear me. Please don't flood."

"Close enough," said Thomas. "But you should actually wear that mask if you mean to speak for the city."

"No," said Rownie, holding up the mask of Zombay but

leaving his own face uncovered. "He has to see that it's me. He has to know that it's me."

The floods pounded against the pylons of the bridge beneath them. Stone creaked against stone. The workings of the clock strained against each other with metallic noises of alarm. Thomas made exasperated noises of his own. "The next line is 'I speak for the city, and all of the city, the north and the south and the bridge in between.'"

"Please don't flood," said Rownie. "For me, and for everyone else, everyone in Zombay."

The River, who was also Rowan, reached down and poked Rownie's nose.

"Nice mask there," he said, with the full roar of the River in the distance of his voice.

Rownie gave him a pirate scowl. "Yours is better," he said.

"Thanks," said Rowan. The lines of the River mask flowed on his face. "Thanks for getting me moving."

Rownie hugged his brother, and his brother hugged him back. "You're welcome. Please don't flood."

"Heard you the first time," said Rowan. "I'll have to leave to manage it, though." He spoke softly, but his voice still thundered.

Rownie wanted to argue. He didn't. He nodded instead. "Will you ever come back?"

Rowan smiled. "You'll know how to find me."

The brothers stood apart. Rowan set both of his hands against the upstream wall. Water flowed from his fingertips and worked its way between the stones, weakening the mortar. Rowan pushed. Several stones tumbled out and down.

Through the open space, Rownie saw the flood. It filled most of the ravine already. Waves tore boulders and trees from the shore on either side.

"Bye," said Rowan, his eyes vast, his hair flowing as though air were water.

"Bye," said Rownie.

His brother jumped over the edge. He cut through the air like a fisherbird, and dove down into the surface of himself.

The troupe gathered beside Rownie. They all watched as the floodwaters calmed, slowed, diminished, and passed beneath their feet and the Fiddleway Bridge.

Act III, Scene X

ROWNIE LEFT THE CLOCK TOWER at evening, a greenish gray pebble in his only pocket. He passed several Fiddleway musicians, more than he had ever seen or heard on the bridge at once, but he was too much inside his own head to really hear the music they played.

He wanted to be alone at his pebble-throwing place, but Vass was waiting for him. She sat on the low stone wall, playing a string game with her fingers. She didn't look up. Rownie climbed the wall and sat beside her.

"Did the Mayor give you your own house?" he asked.

"Oh yes," said Vass. "A dusty and ghoul-haunted place right here on the Fiddleway, and it's all my very own."

"He promised you a house in Northside," Rownie said.

"He did," Vass agreed, "but he's less happy with me now than he was—even though I got him safely through the tunnel. But I don't really mind. I'm not so fond of Northside, and it isn't a bad thing to live in sanctuary. Can't arrest anyone on the bridge."

She got one finger stuck in her string game, and tried to untangle it. She cursed. The web of string turned to ash and blew away. She cursed again, fished more string from a pouch at her belt, and started over. "Speaking of sanctuary, I wouldn't leave the Fiddleway for a while. The Lord Mayor is unhappy with you. I've seen several posters with your face and name."

"I don't have a name," said Rownie. "I only have my brother's name, made small." He said it without any bitterness, but Vass flinched at her own words turned back on her.

"I think it's your name, now," she said.

"Maybe." Rownie looked out at the River, which still flowed higher than its usual custom. "Maybe it is my name." He made it more true by saying it aloud.

Vass got her fingers stuck in the string again. She bit back a curse, and slowly untangled her fingers. She seemed to be struggling with words as much as she struggled with the string.

"I'm sorry," she finally said. "I'm sorry I brought the Mayor and his Captain down on you. I'm sorry about Rowan. I didn't know what they had done to him. I really didn't know. I thought handing you over to the Mayor wouldn't be nearly as bad as what Graba would've probably done to you. I was wrong. I'm sorry."

Rownie looked at her, surprised. "Thanks," he said.

Vass looked at him, and then looked away. "It seems like Graba might actually leave you alone. Southside didn't flood. She'll be happy about that, as happy as she ever gets, and she knows you had some part in it. So she'll probably let you be."

"Good," said Rownie. "I'm glad I don't have to worry so much about pigeons."

The two of them watched the River flow beneath the Fiddleway. Then Vass gave up on her string game, and climbed down from the wall. "I'll be here if you need anything cursed or charmed," she said.

"Good-bye, Vass," Rownie said. "Good luck with the cursing and charming." He almost said *Break your face* instead of *Good luck*, but he thought she might take it wrong.

Once alone, his fingers found the pebble in his coat pocket. He set it on the wall and spun it a few times, like a top. Then he threw the pebble, just to say hello. Rownie watched his brother reach up to catch it.

He climbed down from the low wall and returned to the Clock Tower, through the stable doors that Semele had invited him to see. He returned to learn mask craft and swordplay and all the rest of his new profession. He returned to eat supper.

The tower smelled like cooking. It smelled buttery and good. It reminded him that he was hungry, that hunger followed him always and buzzed behind everything he did. It reminded him that he didn't have to fend for himself here. He took off his brother's old coat as he climbed the stairs and found a costume rack to hang it on. It felt strange to be without it.

Someone—probably Nonny—had put a wood stove outside the pantry and propped up a long metal pipe for a chimney. Cooking smoke climbed the pipe and rose through the tower's workings.

Thomas stood by the stove in an apron. He spooned several dollops of dough onto a flat metal skillet. Semele sat nearby with a book in her hands and her feet on a stool, toes pointed at the stove to soak up its warmth. Nonny, Patch, and Essa all sprawled on the floor, playing cards. Thomas looked up at the boy, grunted, and scooped a finished flatbread onto a plate.

"Don't burn your fingers," the old goblin said.

Rownie took the plate and sat down with the rest of his troupe. His fingers twitched and his mouth watered, but he waited for his supper to cool.

Acknowledgments

AN ENSEMBLE CAST AND CREW created this book, and I am profoundly grateful for the professional, aesthetic, and emotional support I've received along the way.

Thanks to Karen Wojtyla and Emily Fabre for extraordinary and exacting editorial guidance. Thanks to Beth Fleischer, Joe Monti, and Barry Goldblatt for their wise and skillful agenting. Thanks to Holly Black, Kelly Link, and Catherynne M. Valente for nurturing the earliest scribblings set in Zombay. Thanks to Barth Anderson, Haddayr Copley-Woods, David Schwartz, and Stacy Thieszen for encouragement and uncompromising critique. Thanks to professors Phyllis Gorfain, Paul Moser, Roger Copeland, Michael Faletra, Andrew Barnaby, and Richard Parent for their knowledge and willingness to share it. Thanks to the Minnesota State Arts Board, the Minneapolis College of Art and Design, and Rain Taxi for all that they do to support local arts and letters.

Thanks to the master mask makers Bidou Yamaguchi and Jeff Semmerling; both shared essential information about their art, and both have masks named after them inside this book. Thanks to the many astonishing artists who created new masks inspired by my masquerade. Please wander over to goblinsecrets.com to wonder at their work, and to wear it yourself.

Thanks to mis sobrinos Isaac, Navarro, Kyla, and Suzannah for reminding me of so many things I'd forgotten about childhood. Thanks to Melon Wedick, Jon Stockdale, Ivan and Rachel Bialostosky, Nathan Clough, Ahna Brulag, Felicia Batzloff, Will Adams, Matthew Aronoff, Bradford Darling, and to Bethany, Kel, Kay, and Guillermo Alexander. All of them wandered around Zombay and told me things about the place that I didn't know before.

Many thousands of thanks to Alice Dodge for nurturing this book at every stage—and also for marrying me.